Being God

B. A. Binns

Book 2 in the **Farrington Tales** series

Books by

B. A. BINNS

Farrington Tales series

PULL
BEING GOD

Short stories
DIE TRYING AND OTHER STORIES

Being
God B. A. Binns

All The Colors Of Love press
http://allthecolorsoflove.com
facebook.com/allthecolorsoflove

Published by AllTheColorsOfLove
P. O. Box 1583
Arlington Heights, Il 60006
USA

This is a work of fiction. All characters, places and events described are imaginary. Any resemblance to real people, places and events is entirely coincidental.

International Standard Book Number: 978-0-9881821-1-0
ISBN-10: 0988182114
Interior design by Barbara Binns
Editor: Leah Wohl-Pollack, Invisible Ink Editing
First Edition

DEDICATION

Dedicated to my friend Josh, my cover model and inspiration.

CHAPTER 1

On this court, I rule.

Coach Hakeem Kasili divided the basketball team into two squads for today's scrimmage: black against orange. No way will I let black lose. I race for the far end of the court and the expected pass. The moment the ball reaches my hands, I rush the orange-shirted defender positioned between me and my goal. My muscles tighten as I power my way past him and then into the air for the one-handed slam dunk.

The coach, who doubles as the school shrink, blows his whistle and crosses the court toward me. "Don't go crazy out there, Kaplan. This is a game, not war."

He's wrong. Basketball has never been a game. Plus, my life is all about war and I'm done losing. People expect Malik Kaplan to deliver. I expect me to be the best.

I wipe the sweat from my face with the bottom of my black jersey, saying, "Practice makes victorious. Isn't that why we're here?"

"Finesse and intelligence beat brute strength," Coach says. If he were a little shorter I could exchange him and his dark stare for my dad. I never get a "good job" from either of them.

"I scored," I say.

"And nearly injured your teammate doing so."

"My bad, Coach," says Cesare Russo, the forward I barreled through. He and I are the only seniors on our team. He's also one of only two white guys on the squad, if you don't count the light-skinned Hispanics who snarl if you try calling them white. Cesare plays like he's part of the ball, even though he's skinny and twitchy. His orange shirt and the red hair falling in his face make him look like he's on fire.

"You had position, Russo," Coach tells him without turning away from me. "Today's practice is about improving teamwork. I need you to be an example, Kaplan."

"You need me, period."

"The team needs you, but most of all, they need unity. Start working together, or we'll work without you."

"I do my share." *More than my share.*

Kasili starts to say something, then shakes his head and sighs. When he does speak, I know the words are not what he originally intended. "No one manages solo all the time. These guys are your friends, not your enemies."

Yeah, right.

The coach leaves me and goes to talk to his favorite, Julian "The Showboat" Morales. That dumb sophomore does everything except lick the coach's shoes trying to steal my spot as starting center. Morales' old man is up in the stands making a fool of himself with a bunch of other parents who like to come and watch practice. I never have to fear seeing my dad in that rowdy bunch. Sports were never Dad's thing. He barely bothered attending my older brother's football games, and has never come to see me play.

I used to hope to see him come rushing over to me after a game. Seventh grade, eighth, even freshman year, I searched the stands. Julian's father and older brother are always around. Even Cesare's dad shows up when he's in town. He keeps stats and shares his son's glory at every truck stop he visits. Not Dwayne Kaplan. He never pounds my back over a good game or boasts about my points to his employees. He claims being the owner of a growing business takes all his time.

Julian stares at me over the coach's shoulder. He pushes back his long hair, trying to hide his superior attitude.

I wipe my sweaty palms on my shorts and move closer to Cesare. He's bent over with his hands on his thighs, breathing heavily.

"Don't apologize for me," I say. "I charged."

He lifts his head and shrugs. "Chill, man. It's not like this is a real game."

"You should have held the block and stopped me. Don't go messing up now and end up flaking off when it counts. Do your job, or I swear I'll hurt you."

Cesare stares at me as if he sees some creature that doesn't belong on earth, not the guy who kept him from being pounded on in third grade, helped him bury his cat in seventh grade, and taught him the fine art of landing girls in high school. "Play the asshole with others, Malik, not with me," he says.

"I'm not playing, and you know exactly what I am."

"The Badass."

Someone has to be.

After practice, Cesare comes out of the showers fingering the beginner moustache he's grown proud of 'cause his girlfriend calls it cute. He tosses his towel, pulls on a sweater and grins like a crazy monkey. "What say we cruise down State Street, maybe do a little babe-shopping. You game?"

"Your girl won't be happy to hear about your adventures in babe-shopping," I warn.

Cesare's head jerks around like he's scared he'll find his girlfriend, Giselle, standing inside the varsity locker room. "Just a joke, man. You know how I feel about her."

"I know she's got you whipped," I reply. "Running with a guy this whipped hurts my image. Maybe I need a new best friend."

"You find someone you like better than me, just trade me in."

I pull on my camouflage pants and olive gray shirt and grab my M65 camo field jacket. Julian comes into the locker room late, after another talk with the coach. Julian is tall; he's not as tall as me, but few guys are over six-and-a-half feet. Plus, my shoulders are broader, thanks to three years on varsity and forever in the weight room. Julian eyes me as he strips off his orange jersey and flexes his muscles. He's careful not to stare too long or let himself bump me as he brushes past to enter the showers.

The streetlights are on when Cesare and I leave school. He says nothing when I put on my wraparound Ray-Bans. Behind the dark lenses, haters can't see me, but I see everyone and everything.

"What's with the coach and all these extra-long practices?" Cesare says. "And you, Malik, you just kept going and going—what's with that?"

"I like pushing myself. Take vitamins paleface, you dragged on the court."

I'm sky-high as I run into the wind. I could have gone another hour, easy. I'm the captain. I'm taking us to the championship. I don't like the coach, but I agree about the need for extra practice sessions. The sound of wind-whipped flags fills the frigid air. A CTA bus spews black exhaust fumes as it rumbles down the street. A sign on its side holds an advertisement for my father's business. His round face and plastic smile stares out at the streets like some king checking out his turf. Underneath is his slogan, in big black letters: "Kaplan Auto Parts and Body Shop, six Chicagoland locations to serve YOU better."

Right.

If Dad imagines people look up to him, he's wrong. Some street artist turned his glasses into black holes and placed a pitchfork in his folded hands.

My car is a black and silver, personally customized Mustang Boss I saved from the junkyard after my old man declared her unsalvageable. My car is a black and silver, personally customized Mustang Boss I saved from the junkyard after my the insurance company declared her unsalvageable. Her doofus former owner tried drag racing her and tore her apart. Dad bought the wreck, pointed at it, and told me to see what I could do with the pieces. I spent every free minute on her for months, rebuilding the engine and reworking the frame. When I finished she was better than new, with an upgraded engine feeding the wild horses under her hood, the kind that ruled the Old West. I even added a sunroof and painted on racing stripes. In the end I showed him and all the high class mechanics and body men he employs.

Cesare settles into the passenger seat and turns on my radio as I pull out of the parking lot. Bubbly Christmas music pours from the speakers.

"Change stations. It may be December, but dang, I'm already tired of this," I say.

"I like it," Cesare says, but he flips past stations until he finds one of those Complaints-R-Us call-in shows—people yakking about their problems. How City Hall and the mayor's new Urban Management Committee won't give them back lost homes and jobs, or get rid of gangs and fix rotten kids. They even complain about the Chicago Bulls.

"I don't need that crap either," I mutter.

"At least they can't talk about the Farrington Flyers." Cesare laughs as he names our team. "Not after two wins in a row."

The ranting voices fade, and one of Dad's commercials begins playing. I change from the radio to the MP3 player and start up the new release from Enemies of Blood and Flesh. My favorite band doesn't do the happy music thing.

"How do you listen to all this death and destruction and how the world's about to end?" Cesare raises his eyebrows as he looks at me. "We're not emos; at least, I'm not. Anything you're not telling me?"

"My car, my music." *My secrets.*

December in Chicago is always crappy. Snow swirls through the air, heavy enough to make the street slick and people drive like cripples. A girl walks down the slush-filled sidewalk, passing a fake Santa standing in front of a kettle, ringing his bell. A big girl, dressed in a heavy brown coat, with her head bent and a huge purse slung over her shoulder.

Barnetta Murhaselt.

Barney.

She's six feet tall, big and curved, one of the school brains, with no place inside my circle. She is not now, and never has been—well, almost never—one of my ladies. When you're the badass, only hot girls need apply. Not too-smart, big-hipped freshmen whose faces aren't beautiful. Just…interesting.

But Barney is the one that got away, and my nads still tighten with regret.

CHAPTER 2

Every Kaplan who attended Farrington High School dominated sports, controlled the halls, commanded respect, and bore the unofficial title of Badass. That includes my brother, uncle, granddad, cousin, and even a couple of my aunts. Everyone except my dad; he's the forgotten man. There's no mention of Dwayne Kaplan on the school's Wall Of Fame.

This is my year. I'll lead the basketball team to victory and earn my spot in history. A trophy bearing *my* name will be up on the Wall. My older brother Perry lettered all four years and is up there twice for being captain of the undefeated football team his junior and senior years. He was six years older than me, and totally owned himself. I've never matched his brilliance, never made a room light up just by entering the way he did. He did what he chose, when he chose, where he chose. Anyone who dared so much as look at him wrong suffered. The big senior strutted around like he owned every brick, every street, and sure enough every girl. He was the ultimate badass, right until the day he died.

Now there's just me. Now I have to be bad enough for two. I'm not Perry, but I am trying.

These days, people jump for the wall as Cesare and I walk through the halls; bodies shove to the side like cars pulling over for a racing ambulance.

My girlfriend, Nicole Mitchell, leans against my locker, waiting for me when I arrive at school. With a wide, blood-red stripe running through her thick black hair, she's the sexiest girl in school. She has smooth brown skin, red pouty lips, and long slinky hips. Today she wears her orange and black cheerleader top over black skinny jeans. Even guys with girls on their arms track Nicole with their eyes when she walks by. She's a junior who made it her mission to get next to me at the beginning of the semester. And a very pleasant mission it was for both me and Nicole, although there were times when I expected to see a knife sticking out of my former girlfriend's back.

"Where were you last night?" she asks. "I called five times and sent a bunch of texts. You never answered."

"Something came up." Only five? Seemed like more. I stopped checking the phone after her third call and I haven't looked at any of the texts.

"Something more important than me? I don't get you. It's like someone mixed the pieces of two puzzles together to come up with you. And whoever made you left too much that doesn't have a place to fit."

"I fit together fine," I say. She's the one with problems. Next she'll cry. I hate the way she changes from bossy to clingy to tears in seconds. Sometimes she acts like she thinks I don't like her, which is crazy, because what's not to like about Nicole? Maybe she has put on a little weight lately, but even I'm not badass enough to say anything about that. Telling a girl she looks fat is a major female dis; one to avoid unless you're about to dump her. I'm nowhere near done with Nicole. Besides, the girl could use a little meat.

I grab some books from my locker and slam the door shut. "The history teacher got into philosophy yesterday. She wanted a paper on how our 'world views' shaped our choices."

"World view?" Nicole puts a hand on the side of my face. I smell the cocoa butter she uses to keep her skin smooth. "God, Malik, do you even have a world view?"

Of course I do. "Life sucks. The only difference between one day and another is whether or not there's a basketball game at the end." My view of the world is *carpe diem*: grab everything you can reach and hold on tight. I have one choice that matters, the offer from the University of Illinois. This time next year, I'll pound the court as a Fighting Illini and forget all about this school, this place, and my family.

Nicole stares at something over my shoulder and laughs. "Can you believe that girl still comes to school? She's got to be ten months and growing." She steps away from the locker and raises her voice. "Found yourself a desperate drug-head, Shania? How much did you pay to get him to close his eyes and pretend?"

I turn and look at the girl in bulging jeans and a too-long shirt waddling down the hall. She's not the only future mother at school this semester. Some have their noses in the air like they don't care; others hold their heads down, trying to be invisible. They're all laughed at, unless their guy steps up to defend them. Shania keeps her eyes on the floor. Her hunched shoulders and shuffling feet mark her as a target.

Too many kids in this school live to chase targets. I should know. I'm one of them. Looking like a bull's-eye makes us itch to use you for target practice.

I learned my lesson in grade school. Lift your head, stare your enemy straight in the eye, and if he comes close, give a quick shoulder shiver to send him into the lockers. Finish fights before they start or risk getting stomped. Nothing else makes bullies back off.

Even Spencer Shrumm decides to take a shot at the girl. Spencer Shrumm is his real name; it's the kind of thing that would make a guy want to shoot himself. That and the way he can't play football. He's a heavyset junior fullback whose many fumbles and missteps made everyone glad our disaster of a football season finally ended. I almost understand why he sometimes looks so depressed he seems ready to drop in a hole and pull the world on top of him. The guy has done everything but circus tricks to get off the top of Farrington's Most Hated list. His parents left Chicago to visit his sick aunt. He even set up a party for this weekend to help make people forget how he messed up on the field.

This is one of his up days. His eyes glitter with a crazy light. He looks around to make sure people are watching as he says, "They don't print enough money to make a real man touch a great black whale."

Laughter fills the halls. Shania tries moving faster. Spencer steps into her path and their feet tangle.

"Watch it, pig," he says, and gives her a push. She falls against a wall. A water bottle drops from her hand and rolls across the floor until it hits the toe of my gym shoe. Her mouth hangs open like she wants to cry, but nothing comes out. She sniffles and rubs a hand under her nose.

"Do you know any desperate douchebags with bad taste?" Spencer asks, turning a nauseating, slick smile toward me.

I pick up the bottle and throw him the cold, back-the-hell-off look Shania needs to learn. "Right now I see only one douchebag, and he's as brain-dead in the halls as he was on the football field."

"Do you and the great black whale have a little something special going on, Captain Ahab? Maybe you've already reeled her in and now you're just taking care of baby."

My hand tightens around the slick plastic bottle. For a hot second I wonder why he's after me. Lucky for him, his life is saved by the angry, long-haired, six-foot storm in decorated jeans who comes tearing down the hall. Barney's wrists are covered with wide bracelets. She looks fire-hot, with eyes the color of beach sand and black hair tied in a braid that hangs down her back.

The storm points her finger at my chest. I've got six inches on her, yet the tight-lipped scowl she turns on me says she thinks she could take me. If she had a spear, I'd be spareribs.

Me.

It's always me.

I remember the first time I saw Barney, standing in the school cafeteria, looking all tall and cool and delicious. Even though her wide-eyed stare marked her as a freshman, I thought about making her one of my girls. When I walked over to her, something in her face changed, like she'd been lost on Lake Michigan in a storm and I held a life preserver. No girl ever looked at me that way, not before and not since. She's not the normal girl who fits in my arms and makes me feel stronger. But when I put her in the chair next to me that first day, I felt like a superman.

Until her brother arrived. Then we became enemies.

"Leave Shania alone, you…you dork-faced toad." Barney's voice is huskier than I remember, but then she's barely spoken to me since her brother left school a few weeks ago. "I can't understand how even a devil like you goes after someone so helpless."

"'Dork-faced toad.'" Nicole snorts derisively. "That's a real grade school insult."

Spencer snickers. "That the best she can do?"

"I've just gotten started." Barney leans in close, and I smell licorice on her breath. "You're an absolute mindless tool. I mean, if your entire brain was made of cotton you still couldn't come up with enough material to make a panty liner for a dog's pecker!"

Once Barney got past the dork-face thing, she got interesting. I could listen to her voice all day.

"Do you want more?" Barney adds. "Or is the microscopic mote of intelligence floating around in the empty spaces between your ears already overloaded?"

"I'm not the damned devil," I say.

"No. Satan, at least, tried to make something of himself. You're cruel and cold, even to the few people who care about you. You don't like anyone, do you? Not even yourself. Maybe especially not yourself." Barney is shaking as she puts an arm around Shania and leads her down the hall.

Spencer stares at their backs. "Big as that Barn-girl is, I wonder if she's preggers too."

"Barn-girl? Good one," Nicole says. "Malik wouldn't touch either of those clowns."

"He touched one." Spencer points to the water bottle I still hold. "Wonder what else he did."

Not nearly as much as I wanted to with Barney.

The warning bell sounds. Some people head for their first period classes. Some stay, watching and holding their breath, hoping for more. I need to give them something before the wrong rumors start flying.

I step closer to Spencer. "I heard the football coach asked Barney to fill your shoes for that last game."

"Don't start with me." Spencer flexes his muscles, like I couldn't take him down in two seconds. Even Cesare would only need three.

Spencer steps closer, reaching out like he's going to hit me.

If he touches me…if he dares…

I hear the booming voice of Vice Principal Henderson. "What's going on here?"

He crosses his arms over his barrel chest, acting like he's all in charge. Everyone knows the principal would have him for lunch if he ever strayed outside her rules. He's fat, almost as old as my father's father, Waymon Kaplan, and seems like a round dwarf next to me. He looks pale beneath the tan he buys in a can. He probably got punked every day as a kid, so now he gets his jollies from a job that lets him do the punking.

Cesare pushes through the crowd and stares at me, as if trying to use willpower to keep me silent.

"Nothing's going on," I say.

"This does not look like nothing to me," Henderson says.

"Get your eyes checked."

Cesare groans and whispers, "You don't have to fight everyone."

"Really, sir, it's just guy talk," Spencer says. "I was reminding my friends about my party this weekend." He softens his voice and acts the part of model student. I know that role; I've played it a few times myself.

Spencer turns to my girl. "Nicole, don't forget to bring that sister of yours. And bring your scrub buddy, Malik. We'll all have a good time."

He leaves to join the other students hurrying to their classrooms. Nicole follows. I stand my ground.

Henderson steps toward me. "Have you any idea how tired I am of you?" He sounds like the voice taking roll call during detention. I wonder if Henderson is one of the people my dad cheats.

I know there's nothing he can do. If he could kick me out of school he would have done it already. Doesn't matter how tired of me Henderson is. The principal likes me. After all, I come from a long line of school heroes.

CHAPTER 3

The Shrumms need a bigger house." I lean close to Cesare's ear so he can hear me over the noise of dozens of bodies and a really tinny sound system. It's Saturday night. Cesare and I have been at this miserable excuse for a party for almost half an hour.

The music picks up—a salsa beat that pounds at my ears and has the girls kicking off their shoes and forming dance lines. They start stepping. Usually I would stop to watch gyrating hips as the ladies try to outdo each other, but there's no red-striped head in the dance mix. Nicole came with us, but I lost track of her almost twenty minutes ago when I stopped in the kitchen for a beer. Cesare's girlfriend, Nicole's sophomore sister Giselle, is home sick.

It's easy to forget that Cesare is three months older than me, already eighteen. I've spent years on him, but he still doesn't know how to handle girls. He and Giselle have been going together for over a year, but every few months they break it off "forever." Once the breakup only lasted from second to sixth period. Their record is a week apart, set right after homecoming. Even after they fight, she comes back to him. Sometimes I envy Cesare.

Spencer met us at the door with some lame Jekyll and Hyde joke and then disappeared into the crowd. People shove; voices yell. Soon fights will start. Couples are already making out on the stairs of the split-level house. Spencer probably thinks he can keep things contained. I don't think the handwritten "Keep Out" signs he posted on the staircase will protect the upper level much longer.

When I throw a party, cars line the block and fill the driveway and yard of the big house my father built. As long as I don't do anything to bring the cops around, he never bothers to care what I do. By the end of one of my jams, I'm so wasted I barely remember the way to my own bedroom.

I'm not home, so I will have to be a lot more careful tonight.

Cesare and I weave through a crowded kitchen into an even more crowded living room. Chips crunch underfoot. Someone bumps into me, spilling beer down the front of my black polo shirt. I grab at the wet material and glare at the shaking kid. He looks like a freshman. Almost as young as I was the first time my older brother brought me to a high school party. He tries to mumble an apology.

"Down, Jekyll, it was an accident," Cesare says. "Not the first tonight and probably not the last."

"I thought Spencer said I was Hyde," I growl, as the kid rushes back into the crowd.

"Whatever. He's not known for having all lights lit. I still think he was talking 'bout himself. Sometimes that crazy dude plays both roles." Cesare shrugs. "This whole thing sucks. I mean, chips and dip—what does Spencer think we are, eighth-graders? We should leave."

"You just want to leave because Giselle didn't come. At least there's plenty of booze." I finish off my second beer, or maybe it's my third. Who's really counting? I toss the bottle toward an already overflowing garbage can. The bottles inside rattle as I connect.

"Two points," Cesare says.

I laugh and head for the basement. Cesare follows me. There's a second beer stash in a wooden tub filled with ice down there. I need another beer and don't want to face the kitchen mayhem again. There are only a few people in the basement. Unfortunately, Spencer is one of them.

I walk down the creaking staircase and see him standing with a small group of guys. His AstroTurf-green shirt barely covers his stomach rolls.

He laughs and says, "Seriously, the Barn-girl had Malik shaking."

"Oh no." Cesare tries to grab my arm. "Let's go back upstairs."

"Like anyone cares what comes out of the big mouth attached to the useless hands," I say loudly and step forward.

Spencer's head snaps up. "Don't go there."

"Like you didn't go where you were supposed to on the football field?" I say. The tub filled with beer bottles sits in the middle of the room. I dig through the freezing cold, grab a bottle from the bottom, and twist off the cap. One chug sends fire streaming down my throat. I wipe moisture from my mouth with the back of my hand and wait for his next move.

"At least I play on a team where people aren't afraid to hit," Spencer says.

"Do you have a problem with the basketball team?"

"Not the team," Spencer says. "Just the self-appointed god of the court calling himself the captain." He sniffs and runs his hand under his nose, as if wiping away sweat.

Or a booger.

My fingers tighten around the cold beer bottle. I ache to break something, and if that something is a someone, so what? If that someone is Spencer, double points.

Spencer climbs the stairs and disappears. Cesare pulls me back when I start after the ugly fart. "You can't fight everyone who swipes their nose," Cesare says.

"You're not the one he's disrespecting," I say.

"Just don't kill the guy, okay? I don't need blood on my new shirt."

"Like Spencer says, I'm a god, so I get to do what I like." I lift my beer to my lips and have another swallow. I hold the cold bottle against my forehead, but it does nothing for the ache growing behind my eyes. Turning back to the tub, I grab a second bottle and toss it to Cesare.

He shakes his head no. "I had one already."

"I've had…" I pause. I'm not sure how many I've had. "Who's counting? Drink up."

Cesare sighs, takes a swallow, and then follows me back upstairs. People are squashed back-to-chest. Cameraphones are capturing the action. Personal pages on SocialEase and a dozen other social networking sites must already be blazing with the hot footage. Social networking. It's really social dissing. This isn't a party. It's more like an ugly fun house where the floor is at an angle and my legs don't work right.

"Maybe it's good Giselle couldn't come," Cesare says. "She doesn't belong in the middle of this."

"What's so special about her, anyway?"

He gives a jerky shrug. "I love her."

Love?

"Don't say that," I tell him. "When will you learn that girls only get what we're ready to give?" I ask.

"I am so ready to give."

"You're giving her permission to walk all over you. You're a guy, top of the food chain material. Act like it; stay in charge."

"You're just repeating your uncle."

Who else should I repeat? My dad?

"Uncle Leon knows all about women. He knows how to make women respect him." He's a fun guy; he makes everyone laugh and tells great stories. He has my granddad's take-no-stuff-from-no-one attitude. He can grow so fire-hot only a fool would refuse to back down when he's mad. He's totally different from my plastic father. My dad just gets all quiet and cold, like some toy soldier frozen in wax.

"I don't want Giselle's respect," Cesare says. "I want her to love me."

"Look, she's not here; you're free tonight. Freer than I am." I look around. Where the hell is Nicole, anyway? "Relax and drink your beer," I tell Cesare. "I'm going to find Nikki."

He looks at his bottle and shrugs. "I told you, I don't like the taste."

"What has taste got to do with anything? You come to a party; you're supposed to have fun."

My favorite song flows through the speakers. Horst, the lead singer for Enemies Of Blood and Flesh, begins one of their sexiest ballads, "You And Me And The Night."

I need Nicole. This is our song.

I push through the crush and enter another room, where I see Spencer seated on a sofa. Nicole sits beside him. No, not beside. He's halfway on top of her, with one arm across her shoulders and his head on her chest like she's some kind of body-pillow. One hand hangs from her shoulder, waves in the air maybe a half-inch from her breasts. His other hand rubs her bare knee. She giggles like she enjoys having him wrapped around her.

"Nikki." I push people aside, cross the room, and slap his hand away from her breast. She jumps to her feet and throws her arms around my neck. Spencer remains on the sofa, looking up with a smirk twisting his lips.

"Why'd you let that lowlife crawl all over you?" I ask Nicole. I free myself from her hold. "How's that make me look?"

"We were only talking. I've been looking all over for you and got tired. I sat down to rest my feet and Spencer stopped to talk. You know you're my only." She walks her fingers down my chest as she talks. The move used to get me hot, but right now it bugs me almost as much as the lopsided grin on Spencer's face.

Horst's mellow bass voice sings:

"We alone tonight.

"You and me, tonight.

"Nothing stops us babe, no one home."

"Come with me." I take her arm and pull her away from the room. I push my way through the crush, past the dancers, up the stairs, ignoring the ridiculous Keep Out signs, and into one of the forbidden bedrooms. Once inside, I turn on the light. This must be Spencer's parents' room. They are definitely not neat freaks; the place is almost as messy as my bedroom. The king-sized bed is unmade. A pair of striped boxers lies on the floor next to a frilly red nightgown and heeled shoes.

Leaving the door open so we can still hear the music, I walk up behind Nicole, put my arms around her, and bend close while singing along with Horst.

"'You know what we feel.

"'It's all good, so real.

"'You know what comes next, we're alone.'"

She squirms free just before I can plant a kiss on her neck. She moves fast, like one of the lean, mean cats haunting alleys; the ones who know every survival trick ever invented.

"I hate that song." She pretends to snarl. Her tight lips and narrowed eyes make her look just like her mother.

"You love that song," I remind her.

"No, *you* love that song." She swats my hand away when I reach for her again. "Is sex all you can think about?"

I guess her snarl wasn't pretense. "That's why I brought you up here. This is the kind of one-on-one I'm in the mood for."

"What if it's not what I'm in the mood for?" Her jaw clenches tighter than any trash-talking pro wrestler. "Basketball and sex, that's all you ever think about. Do you even care about me?"

"You're my girl." What more does she want? "I've got condoms. Like the song says, you know what comes next."

"There's more to going together than you grabbing me. I love you, Malik. Do I mean anything to you?"

WTF?

Nicole wants to do the do-you-love-me thing now.

Now?

"How about you give me a little respect?" she insists, crossing her arms over her chest and lifting her chin like a soldier on the battlefield.

Horst's voice grows louder, asking his girl to please, please, *please* stay with him. I'm not making that mistake. I won't beg. And I won't force her.

"You pushed your way into my life," I say. "Don't complain because you got exactly what you asked for."

She walks out, slamming the door behind her.

CHAPTER 4

I drop down on the unmade bed. A few minutes later, the door opens and Cesare steps in. He holds his still-full bottle and looks worried.

"Nicole's upset," he says.

"What do you think I am?"

"We need to leave. Come on, we'll collect her and go home."

"I don't want to go home." I take a swallow from my beer and feel the familiar rush. I don't want him making excuses for my girl. He needs to keep watch over his own business. "There's a reason Giselle isn't here tonight."

"Don't start on her just because you're having a problem with Nicole. They're sisters, but they're nothing alike."

"Damn right they're not. Did you really believe the headache thing?"

"Stomachache." His voice grows loud, as if trying to convince me that Giselle's reason for not coming with him actually matters. He steps further into the room and shuts the door behind him, closing out the sounds of the party.

"Don't you get that she doesn't want to be here with you?" I ask. "I bet you've never even done her. Is that why you keep hanging on her tail and letting her boss you, because she says no?"

His jaw clenches. "Hasn't any girl ever said no to you?"

His words strike a blow, sending more memories surging through my head. I drop my bottle and leap from the bed. Beer soaks into the pillows.

"Sorry, I forgot," Cesare says.

He *forgot?* Nobody forgets.

Everyone at school knows how the badass of Farrington High lost not one but two girlfriends, bang-bang, just like that. Not because Barney walked out on me—no one believes I ever really wanted a nobody like her. Not even because her brother David stole my former girlfriend. People don't forget because of what *I* did when I went after Barney to hurt him, and he retaliated against me.

I forgot what I was, and who I was.

The bullies outside my house never matched the one who lived with me. I learned to be afraid, even in my own house. Perry never stopped until he made me beg. My body learned to go on automatic.

No parents around plus Perry in a rage equals pain, until Malik leaks enough tears to satisfy the older brother.

After he died, I thought the danger was gone. My body grew, muscles and bone. I thought nothing would ever reduce me to that. Until Barney's brother came after me. He stood over me, threatened me, and the autopilot took over. Inside my head, it was me and Perry all over again.

Barney's brother took pictures of me on the ground, sniveling like a kid. Those pictures raced around the Internet, making me a thousand-hit wonder and leaving me the nickname Booger Kaplan, the man I will *never* let myself be again. I still fight like hell to beat down that name. I see the sideways looks. I see people turn and stare when I walk down the street and wonder if they recognize me from the pictures. I won't get that low again. Not for any reason.

I need more beer. I came to this stupid excuse for a party to drink. This stuff makes my problems disappear. Makes me disappear too.

I grab Cesare's bottle and drink deep, and the world changes. Something inside me turns off; I enter zombieland, and it's not a movie.

"I'm not ready to go," I say, when the bottle in my hands is as empty as the one lying on the bed. "I need more beer."

"Maybe you're drinking too much," Cesare says.

"Maybe you're in my business too much."

The bedroom door opens again. This time Spencer steps into the room, bringing the scent of weed with him. "What are you two doing in here all alone?" He shuts the door behind him and looks from Cesare to me to his parents' bed. A cold, nasty smirk twists his lips. "Are you having some kind of personal get-together?"

"Back off or prepare for pain." I really hope he's as dumb as he looks and doesn't listen.

"Just joking." He lifts a hand to display a bong. "Come on, guys, smoke the peace pipe with me."

"I don't smoke that crap," I say.

Spencer turns to Cesare. My friend shakes his head and says, "No."

"No. Or not with me?" Spencer asks dryly.

"Both," Cesare says.

Spencer shakes himself and turns to me. "You still out to bang the Barn-girl?"

I almost choke, but bite down the acid rising in my throat.

Cesare laughs. "Malik never liked her, you idiot. He pretended to date her as a fake-out."

"I've seen him stare after the girl in school." Spencer keeps looking at me. "Makes no sense when you've got one of the fine Mitchell sisters."

I follow Cesare's lead. "Do you think I'm crazy enough to choose some big, hippy, too-smart-for-her-own-good freshman over Nicole top-of-the-cheerleader-pyramid Mitchell?"

"I think you're lucky. Or at least Cesare's lucky. You have your dad's money to thank for the cheerleader."

"Shut up," Cesare says.

"Mr. Kaplan has all the money in the world," Spencer continues, his voice gruff and bitter. "Gave Malik a car. Damn fine car, too."

"It was a totaled wreck I rebuilt," I say.

"You rebuild your clothes too? And your wallet? That's why girls slobber over you and give you what you want."

Spencer takes another hit before staggering across the room to stand inches from Cesare. "Your scrub buddy, on the other hand—what's he got to offer? Maybe his old man will bring a few extra oranges when he trucks back from Florida, or wherever the hell he's hauling now. That'll attract the ladies."

Cesare's cheeks flush pink. "I'm outta here." He starts for the door.

"No, stay. Take a toke." Spencer moves into Cesare's path, forcing him to step backward.

"I told you no."

"White boy doesn't want what I have to give?" Spencer's eyebrows lift and his thick lips curl over clenched teeth. "Too good to join me? You can chase a sister but look down on me when I try treating you like a brother?"

"If you're pissed at me, Spencer, just come after me," I say.

"It's not always about you, Malik," Spencer says. He barely glances in my direction. "Come on, Cesare; prove you're one of us."

Cesare's breathing grows rapid but this time, he accepts the bong.

"Don't do it," I say. "You don't even like that shit."

"I don't like beer either, but you're always after me to drink," Cesare says.

As he puffs, Spencer says, "Tell me, what's it like for you, slumming with the black girl because your own kind won't have you?"

"Kind of like you feeling up on my leftovers," I say, and shake my head. The world spins and I grab the headboard for support. I open the sliding glass doors that lead to the balcony and let cold air sweep my face.

"Tell me about the Mitchell sisters," Spencer says. "Do you two switch off sometimes? Or does Nicole refuse to leave the money man?"

That's twice now he's talked about my dad's money, like I can't do anything on my own.

"What girl would hang with Booger Kaplan if she didn't expect to get something out of the deal?" Spencer laughs.

I'm halfway across the spinning room by the time Cesare grabs my arm to stop me. "Don't let him get to you," Cesare says. "He's high, that's all. Let's just get Nicole and get out of here," Cesare says.

"Nikki follows the dollar signs." Spencer points a finger at Cesare. "As for you…" He pauses. "Your girl's the kind who likes rooting around with the other white meat."

Cesare releases me and lunges for Spencer. I fall on the bed. Cesare's fist connects with Spencer's jaw. The cigarette flies across the room and lands on my arm. I brush it aside just as the lit end begins to burn my skin.

A lamp crashes to the floor. The bulb explodes; shards of glass cut into my arm. One of them, maybe Cesare, maybe Spencer, I'm too dizzy to be sure, rushes through the open doors to the balcony. The other one follows. I hear a crash.

I stagger across the room and step out on the balcony. It's empty too. Below I see a stand of snow laden bushes that broke their fall. Branches are bent and broken. Spencer lies on the ground. Cesare is on top of him, fists pounding his face. Spencer moans, but barely moves or tries to block Cesare's blows.

I lick the back of my hand and taste salt and the bitter, metallic syrup of blood. I remove a shard of glass from my arm before leaping over the porch rail to the ground. Cesare's flying fists land a blow on the side of my jaw as I pull him away from Spencer. It's almost funny. Cesare is always the one calming me down. Now he's out of control.

"You won," I say. "He's down."

Down and moaning as the front door opens and kids pour from the house. Sirens announce approaching police cars.

"We have to go. Now," I say, but Cesare won't listen. He keeps struggling to free himself from my grip. I hear screams and running feet. Cars start. Girls squeal. By the time Cesare stops fighting me, it's too late. The cops are here. They do their usual, grabbing every moving body they corner and hauling us all off to the one place I've escaped until now.

Jail.

CHAPTER 5

N
o sound rips your guts like the clang of a lock turning in a jail cell door.

Cesare paces our cell. His hair sticks to his sweaty forehead as he moves—nine steps one way, nine the other. Part of me wants to tell him to sit down; most of me wants to join him.

This place is nothing like what I see on cable. They never show water dripping over the sides of the clogged toilet and running across the stone floor to the smelly drain hole. On TV, you don't hear voices moaning or cursing or taunting, and you can't tell how creepy it feels to have so many eyes staring at you.

A thick, bald guy in the next cell stares at us like he sees something fascinating.

At me. He's staring at me.

He doesn't seem the kind of guy who'd spend a lot of time online, but you can never tell. He looks our age. The tattoos on his head and neck brand him as a member of the Graveyard Enforcer gang. More than a member—he must have a high rank to earn the deep claw marks slicing across his crooked skull. As he scrunches up his face, I take a deep breath, preparing for the worst; he's probably searching what passes for his brain, seeking the memory of where he's seen me before and what I was doing. I can stare back, or I can act like he's nothing—too unimportant for me to care about. I turn my back on him and look at Spencer.

He grips the bars on the cell door, as if holding the pieces of black metal will somehow make them melt away. He shakes like a wino in winter. One of his eyes is swollen. Someone slapped a bandage on the gash on his face. Cesare looks worse; he was at the bottom when they fell off the porch. When the police shoved us in the van, Spencer screamed about a concussion and swore his leg was broken.

"I'm gonna die. My dad will kill me," Spencer moans.

"Suck it up and act like a man," I say. No father nerdy enough to drop a name like Spencer Shrumm on his only kid is going to kill him. Not even when he gets home and sees how badly his house was trashed. He'll want that kid alive and suffering.

"Easy for you, Malik. Your old man never even cares what you do."

Not true. Oh, he won't yell or curse, won't say much of anything at all. He'll just hand me that familiar, unforgiving steel glare through his thick glasses.

"I'm sick of your whining," the dude in the next cell says. His voice sounds like he swallowed gravel and he needs a little of our blood to wash the mess down. "Shut up, or I'll rip you to pieces."

I'm sick of Spencer too, but tonight it's us against the Enforcer. I step closer to the bars. "You want to hurt one of my guys, you better bring an army."

"That dude smells worse than the toilet," Spencer says. "What do you think he's in for? Bet he killed someone."

I'd guess drugs, God's little multicolored treats for the world. But murder works too. Explains how he earned a cell all to himself.

Spencer comes closer to me, careful to keep me between him and Cesare. The move puts him close to the bars between the cells. The Enforcer reaches through those bars and grabs him in a headlock. Voices from surrounding cells laugh and call out encouragement as Spencer struggles to breathe. The guy whispers something in Spencer's ear. Spencer stops struggling and goes perfectly still, like a mouse hypnotized by a torturing cat.

I go after the Enforcer, hitting him once, twice. My knuckles burn and split. I'm pulling back for a third strike when the guy releases his hold and Spencer falls free.

"That was fun," the Enforcer says. Spencer limps across the cell to a metal bench attached to the wall. The Enforcer still stares at me, only now it seems like he's trying to memorize my face. "I like you, man.

Are you connected?"

"No way." I could name my dead brother, or my uncle who still keeps contact with his old friends from the gang, even the ones in jail. Or Granddad, the neighborhood's original badass. But I don't.

"You should be." He rubs the side of his face. "You've got brains, guts, and loyalty to your man. You belong with your brothers."

I've sat through anti-gang lectures ever since grade school. A few months ago, Kasili came out with a lot of crap, claiming, "They're not heroes, not even anti-heroes, just punks. Someday they'll get what they deserve." He didn't know how much those words made me hungry to run with the Enforcers. Sometimes I feel like sliding up to some of the guys I see controlling the streets and saying, *Hey, I'm yours.*

I back away from the pull of this Enforcer's words and move to stand in front of Cesare. I'm not worried about the Enforcer, my dad, or Spencer. I worry about Cesare. He's in real danger.

I felt lucky that sunny day in third grade when I saw the school bully cornering the new kid. The bully looked up from taunting Cesare and saw me. I felt the wheels turn in his head as he argued with himself about going after his usual target or sticking with the kid he had. He made his decision and turned his back on me. I was safe, and headed for home.

But before I had gone a block the sun clouded over, the back of my neck itched like crazy, and for some reason, my feet turned and took me back. Cesare and I put the bully down together and from then on, we were a team.

Within weeks, the whole school knew the penalty of messing with the black-and-white-brothers. I protected Cesare from guys who thought a white kid didn't belong in our neighborhood. He protected me from having no one.

If I have to, I'll protect him again.

"Relax," I tell him.

"I'm fine."

"Your cheeks are beet red; it's a dead giveaway. Stop worrying, I'll tell them this was all on me."

He shakes his head. "You can't do that. I'm the one who tore Spencer up."

"I'd have beaten the hairy snot myself if you hadn't jumped him first. A record now will kill your chance of being recruited. No scholarship, no college. It can't be you. You'll be nailed to the damn wall."

Cesare has had trouble before. His seventh grade sister was bullied last year. The guy followed her home and threatened to hurt her. Cesare didn't try to hide what he did to the guy; he wanted people to know the penalty for messing with a Russo. The bully's old man screamed about hate crimes to reporters. But that fight wasn't about black and white—it was about family. Most people around here understood, and hardly anyone paid attention when the media came and tried to make it into some big deal. I told Cesare to let me handle things next time.

"You don't need another set of parents screaming 'hate crime' at you," I remind him.

"I do hate that fucktard." He points at Spencer.

"You and me both. But we have to play it this way."

"You can't take the blame for me."

"I can. People will believe it too." People believe anything bad about me, and they're usually right. What's the point of having a rep if I don't use it? Thanks to the Enforcer, my knuckles are bloody. That will make my version more believable.

"Don't worry, I'm still seventeen; I have nothing to lose. They'll go easy on me. Dad will just open that hefty wallet Spencer talked about and pay the fine. At worst, it's a few days out of school. No biggie. I could use the vacation. You wanted to leave, I made us stay, so this is my fault. Now I end this."

I take a seat on the bench next to Spencer. Cold seeps up from the metal and through my jeans. Cesare stands beside me, arms crossed, with a sullen expression on his face.

"Here's how this will go," I say. "Cesare wasn't part of what went down. He wasn't in the fight."

"He started the fight," Spencer growls.

"Your mouth and your pot started the fight," I remind him.

"Meaning what?" Spencer points at the marks on his face. "You expect me to say I did this to myself? No way. Somebody has to pay."

"Meaning I'm the one who beat the crap out of you. You'll tell it the way I say, or I'll make it the truth."

Spencer looks across at the Enforcer and shrugs, his resistance suddenly fading. "You want to suffer for him, go for it."

A half hour passes. We practice our stories until the door to the outside opens. I see three cops. One stands beside the outer door. The others cross the chamber toward our cell. The younger of the two is probably a rookie. He doesn't look much older than me and swaggers forward with one thumb stuck in his belt. His other hand holds a set of handcuffs.

The Enforcer lunges at the bars as the cops pass his cell. The rookie jumps back and drops the handcuffs as he struggles to keep his balance. The metal clangs as the shackles hit the dirty, gray stone floor, and the Enforcer laughs. The older cop looks like he's fighting to keep from laughing, too, as his partner retrieves the cuffs and steps to our cell door.

"Malik Kaplan, front and center." The rookie's voice is so shaky, I bet he bit his tongue.

I take my time rising. "The name's pronounced Mah-Leek. Say it right."

His fist tightens until his knuckles grow pale. "I don't care if you're called Leaky-leaky; don't give me trouble. You come to the door. The rest of you stay back."

The Enforcer laughs again. "Leaky-leaky."

I've been called worse. Guess he didn't see the pictures after all.

The cops take me into an office where my dad and his lawyer wait.

Dad stands with his hands thrust deep into his coat pockets, chatting with the cops about his disappointment of a son. He isn't a short man, but I grabbed a bunch of height genes. He has to look up to meet my eyes, something he rarely bothers doing. Under his coat I see a dark suit and tie. You'll never find him out of uniform, not even in a police station at two in the morning. His hair is heavily laced with some anti-gray formula he buys from a corner shop in Chinatown. He swears by that kind of offbeat crap. Dad cultivates the oily snake look, claiming customers expect that. He's the perfect businessman who makes money just by breathing and cheating customers. He started with cars, and now he's moving into real estate. His dark brown eyes are constantly measuring, evaluating, rejecting.

Sometimes I just want him to see me. To forget my brother and think that maybe I'm the son he always wanted, instead of the second stringer he's forced to make do with. Not like this, though. I hate the look in his eyes when he finally lifts his head and stares at me and the handcuffs. Something about his face—too calm, too tight—makes me think of the hyper kids who sell their Ritalin in the moments just before they explode because they can't handle class. Perry used to laugh about Dad being forever on his case. I sat back and watched and envied the way my brother always made the man jump through hoops.

No hoops for me. Just silence.

His lawyer, Zachery Patterson, a short man with bushy eyebrows and sand-colored skin, looks more the fatherly type than my dad. He smiles at me, waves me over, talks to me. I wish he were my father; I need someone who doesn't make me feel like a failure.

Mr. Patterson keeps advising me about that remain silent thing, saying I should let him do the talking. It almost hurts to ignore his advice. If he were my father, maybe I would change my mind and my plans. But my dad remains silent, so I insist on telling the cops the version of the night's events I prepared.

I wonder what Dad would do if he knew the planning that went into my confession. Would he be proud and say, *Great thinking, son?*

Or wash his hands and tell the cops, *Enough—you can keep him?*

CHAPTER 6

It's almost dawn before the paperwork is done and we get to leave. The sky is too cloudy for stars; even the moon is barely visible. My father is silent as we exit the police station. He walks in front of me, doesn't even look back to make sure I'm following. Our steps crunch on packed snow as we walk to the old sedan he's had for most of my life. I settle into the passenger seat and stare out the window. He starts the car and pulls out of the parking lot so fast that I'm pushed deep into the cushions.

I don't expect him to say much. Even after Perry died, all he did was shake his head and say, *Don't do drugs.* But surely a pre-dawn trip to jail will force him to talk to me. I wonder if he'll stutter, or repeat himself—even raise his voice.

He drives in silence for several blocks. Then his hands tighten on the steering wheel. "I can't believe you were out drinking," he says.

"I only had a couple of beers."

"A couple? That's the lie every drinker tells. You're underage. You shouldn't have had any alcohol."

"Just because you don't know how to have fun…"

"Fun? Have you learned nothing from watching your grandfather? What were you thinking?"

"I wasn't."

He frowns like I said something that hurt him and slams on the brakes. The seat belt digs into my chest as we lurch to a stop.

"Watch it, old man," I say when the tires stop squealing. "Maybe I should take the wheel. You could get us killed driving like that."

He presses his fingers over his eyes. I wonder if his head aches the way mine does.

"When does it end, Malik?" he asks.

Good question. I have no answer.

I turn and stare out the window.

"Do you have any idea how much damage you did?"

"It wasn't all me." I snap my lips shut. I can't use the SODDI defense—some other dude did it. Not when that dude is Cesare.

"You'll have to go to court," Dad says. "Patterson is sure he can work out some kind of deal."

He doesn't sound happy about that.

"I'm sleepy." I yawn and stretch and close my eyes. "Let's get home."

We reach the shopping district, where sale signs beg window-shoppers to enter and spend big. Darkened stores with boarded-up windows warn people what will happen if they don't spend. Foreclosure signs in front of houses and apartment buildings explain why people can't. Dad drives until we reach a red light. Ours is the only car around, people around here learn the Life-In-The-Hood lessons young and stay close to home after dark. Dad waits for the light to change. We sit in font of a vacant lot filled with broken bottles and busted bricks, a good place to keep your ass away from. Even street people possess the sense to hang somewhere else.

A group of guys stands near the corner, just outside the light cast by the streetlamp. You don't live your life in this part of Chicago without knowing the signs. I can tell by the way they stand and dress that they are the real deal. Enforcers. Maybe lost souls searching for their jailed lieutenant.

The Graveyard Enforcer gang used to be powerful around here, but police and community leaders have pushed back on their illegal activities. Granddad sometimes gets all mournful and claims they are just a shadow of what they once were. Still, these are the guys no one likes, but everyone respects. The kind of people that would make Mom renew her attempts to make Dad move. Guilt makes him give in to her about everything—everything except leaving.

Dad never turns his head to look at the group. Like everyone else who calls himself a respectable citizen, he pretends not to notice trouble in the hope that trouble will be just as blind to him. The light turns green and he guns the motor. I thought he liked the old car.

Four more blocks and we drive past the Shrumm house. The lights are out, hiding the damage. My Mustang Boss is still parked down the block.

"Hold up, we have to go back and get my car," I say.

Dad doesn't slow down. "You're not driving anywhere tonight."

I shrug and settle back. "Fine, I'll come back for her tomorrow."

"No. You could have climbed behind the wheel and earned yourself a DUI, or hurt someone."

"But I didn't."

"And you won't. You no longer have a car."

"You can't take my car." She's my personal concept car. Dad may have paid for the parts, but *I* did the work.

A muscle twitches in Dad's jaw. "The name on the title is Dwayne Kaplan. You're going to need to pay damages; the sale of the car will make a good start."

"Sale?" I hate him. I swear I do. The title may read Dwayne Kaplan, but I sweat and bled over that car. "Money. That's all you care about."

"Maybe it's time you learned to care about money a little more. This isn't open for discussion; the car is gone. In addition, there are new rules. From now on, you will be home by curfew."

"I don't have a curfew."

"You do now. You'll be home by ten on school nights."

"I'm not a child."

He pulls into his spot inside our garage, turns off the motor, and says, "This is my house. While you live here, you live by the rules I set."

His house. His car. But I'm his son. Maybe the second son, but Perry is gone. Don't I count for something?

I don't care. I don't.

I won't let myself care.

"Maybe I won't live here anymore." *Is that it? Does he want me gone?* He hasn't been like this since the night he tried to ground Perry. Look how well that worked out.

"Feel free to make that choice whenever you wish," he says, before disappearing inside the house.

For a moment, I almost admire my dad.

Almost.

CHAPTER 7

After a night in jail, I thought I'd be happy to be home. But after three days stuck at home, the place feels a lot like that cell.

I was charged with a felony: aggravated battery. Schools don't like felons prowling the halls. That means I'm suspended. Henderson must be dancing. There's talk of an expulsion. I saw the email the school sent Dad. I cracked the password on his home computer years ago and he never changed it.

A blue spruce Christmas tree fills half our living room, and two candles burn in the *chanukiah* here in the dining room, a menorah with nine branches instead of the usual seven. One of the burning candles represents today, and the other is the *shamesh*, the server candle used to light it. Today is the first day of Chanukah, the eight-day festival of lights I used to confuse with Christmas. I mean I have a Catholic mother and a Hebrew Israelite father. Neither one is all that heavy into religion—what did they expect? I was almost six before I really understood there was a difference between Mom lighting up a tree and singing hymns, and Dad lighting candles and chanting prayers.

Chanukah celebrates an old battle where the Jewish Maccabees proved that force works. Those guys put the hammer down and bitch-slapped a bunch of ancient Greeks, and now we celebrate for eight days each year. Chanukah isn't even one of the big Jewish holidays, but my otherwise secular Hebrew Israelite father makes these eight days a big deal. He only goes to Temple Beth Shalom for the high holidays. He mostly just writes big checks for the rabbi so he can keep calling himself a member. He did insist I have a Bar Mitzvah after Mom took me to First Communion. These days, I don't go near either church or synagogue. Like Dad, I stopped the hypocrisy right after Perry's funeral. But after Dad chanted the praises and lit the candles, I sent up a silent prayer. *Really God, I could use something a little stronger than coffee to help me get through this evening.*

I sit at the dining room table with my parents and Mr. Patterson, the lawyer. The smell of garlic and celery fills the air. Mom cooks when she's upset. She wears a brown dress. She always wears neutral colors, things she hopes will make people overlook her. My mom is beautiful, barely forty, and when she walks around, even young guys give her a second look. At least they do until they see the scars.

Dad worked as a mechanic, but with two kids to feed, Mom needed to work too. Until the day an oven exploded in the restaurant where she waitressed. The flames left her with an insurance settlement that financed the rise of the Kaplan empire. It also cost her three fingers and left scars on her right arm, shoulder, and the side of her face. Even after twelve years and a ton of operations, some mornings the scarred skin tightens up, and I see her grit her teeth to keep from crying when she moves.

She seldom leaves the house except to attend Mass. When she does go out, she pulls on a scarf and gloves, and wears long sleeves and a high collar. She prays, takes communion, and lights candles for my dead brother—all with her right hand hidden in her pocket.

The plastic surgeon couldn't give her the miracle I prayed for. It doesn't matter what name I call him, or what church I try, God remains super-selective about answering my calls.

I look down at the pasta and giant meatballs staring back at me from my plate. Dad sits across from me. He leans back in his chair with his hands thrust deep in his pockets. I'm not fool enough to believe his grin means he's happy. He uses that same plastic smile when irate customers or suppliers come charging into his office. They never leave with what they wanted. Mom sits beside me, being careful to keep her left side facing the lawyer. He's the only one who eats, shoving pasta into his gaping, killer whale mouth.

"I want this nightmare to be over," Mom says. "My son cannot go to prison."

Dad and I stare at each other. Mom thinks miracles happen if you just say the right words the right way. Her easy assumption that the world will work as she commands unites Dad and me for a second.

Then the second passes and he looks away.

"I'm doing my best, Mrs. Kaplan," Mr. Patterson says between bites.

"Boys fight all the time," Mom says. "What Malik did was wrong, but it was just child's play."

"It's called battery, Celeste," Dad says.

Mom's right hand reaches across the table before she catches herself and grabs his arm with the hand that works. The scars only make her face interesting. Doesn't she see? Doesn't Dad tell her?

"I lost one child," Mom says. "I won't have the other in prison. You can't let that happen."

Mr. Patterson downs spaghetti while nodding to Mom. "The good news is the Shrumm boy's injuries weren't serious, and the DA agreed to reduce the charges from aggravated to simple battery."

Instead of using her don't-talk-with-your-mouth-full glare on him, Mom bites her lip. "What exactly does that get us?"

He points his fork at me. "It gets Malik a Class A misdemeanor. That keeps us out of adult court and takes prison off the table."

"Just what *is* on the table?" Mom asks.

"Simple battery, disturbing the peace, and vandalism." He takes another bite. "At most, a six-month sentence."

Six months. In another cell with an overflowing toilet and the smell of old vomit and stale urine. A cell where we prisoners stare at each other, and wait for someone to make the first wrong move. A lot like the school halls.

"I told you—no prison." Mom's fingers curl tightly.

Dad grips her hand. "He won't have to go to prison. Six months means jail."

"Your husband is right, Mrs. Kaplan." The lawyer nods at my dad.

"What's the difference?" I say. "A cell's a cell."

"The difference is the kind of company you'll find yourself with," Dad says.

Patterson grins like Dad is some star student. "Right again, Mr. Kaplan. Prison is a whole other world. Malik doesn't belong there, even though his little confession almost landed him inside. Do you know how hard that made my job, young man?"

"I'm man enough to admit what I did." I made things easy for Cesare. The charges against him were dropped. Spencer got an actual apology when his parents threatened false arrest. Cesare didn't get the apology, but he keeps a clear record.

"Malik felt remorse. That's the one good sign in this episode." Dad nods as he speaks.

"Not remorse." I don't realize I'm speaking out loud until his look of approval fades. My lips tighten, but I wouldn't snatch the words back if I could.

"Don't bring that attitude in front of the judge." The lawyer rubs the back of his neck. "You'll want to spread buckets of remorse."

"Being phony helps?"

"Letting the court know you're sorry helps. Making the judge believe you won't engage in this behavior again helps. Otherwise we could lose this deal."

Mom turns to him so quickly her hair flies away from her face. "You have to keep that from happening."

"I'm trying, Mrs. Kaplan." Patterson blinks, but he doesn't look away from the exposed scars.

"Try harder. My husband is paying you a fortune. Take care of my son. His confession shouldn't matter—he's only a child."

"I'm not a child." My fingers tighten around my fork until the grooves on the handle dig into my palm. First Dad and a curfew, now Mom calling me a kid. What do I have to do to show them I'm a man? The Enforcer in the cell gave me more respect than my parents do.

The steely-eyed lawyer looks at me and nods as if he hears my thoughts. "Your son is correct. In the eyes of the law, seventeen is more than old enough for him to choose to waive his Miranda rights and speak for himself."

"Youth is not a 'get out of jail free' card, Celeste," Dad says.

"Is that an Urban Management philosophy?" Bitterness colors her voice. "Our son is more important than some speech for the mayor."

"This has nothing to do with politics," Dad says.

Liar. Dad wants our alderman to recommend him for a position on the mayor's new committee. I know that's why he wants Patterson to settle things quickly and quietly. He wants me and my troubles hidden out of the way.

"At least the technicality of Malik being a juvenile works in our favor," Patterson says.

"Does that mean I go to juvie?" Not good, but not really so bad. I know guys who've spent time there, and they say it's no big deal. Except for the small rooms and hard beds, the early morning wake-up calls, the bad food, the fences, and the guards. And the boredom. I set my fork down beside my knife. The imprint of the handle still shows in my palm. *This is my choice*, I remind myself. Things are worse than I thought they would be, but not as bad as they could be.

I turn to Mr. Patterson. "What would have happened if I were eighteen?"

He drops his fork on his empty plate and wipes his face with a napkin. "Misdemeanor or not, your case would be handled in adult court, and the prosecutors there are very hardnosed."

"So it would have been really bad." I breathe deep, knowing I made the right choice.

"Maybe even that prison thing your mother worries about. But everyone, relax," the lawyer adds before Mom can speak. "We kept this in juvenile court and I have very good connections there. Your father is right; the biggest thing will be the monetary issue. You'll have to pay for repairs to the house and the boy's medical bills."

"They have insurance."

"That doesn't lower your liability." Patterson scowls. "Expect a hefty fine, too. The district attorney will also want community service in exchange for probation. That won't leave you with much time to work to pay what you'll owe."

"Well, if that's all, then there's no trouble." Mom smiles as if the bad dream is over.

"I'll have plenty of time to work since I'm being expelled from school," I say, when Dad remains silent.

Mom's head jerks. "What now?"

"The school wants me gone."

Dad shifts in his chair. "I received word that the administration has started expulsion proceedings. But now that the charges have been reduced to a misdemeanor, I'm sure that will change."

"That school is lucky to have my son," Mom says. "We should

have sent him to private school, the way I wanted. Maybe we can still—"

Dad shakes his head. "Malik can't just run away from his problems."

"People do it all the time," I say.

"'Ask not for a lighter burden but for broader shoulders,'" Dad says, quoting from one of his tired Jewish proverbs. Guess he doesn't notice my shoulders are way broader than his.

Mom pats my arm. "Do you want to stay at that school?"

"Yes."

"Then that's it, Mr. Patterson." She waits for the lawyer to look back at her. "Go to the school and tell them our son stays."

"I'm a criminal attorney, Mrs. Kaplan. Negotiating with schools is a little outside my area of expertise."

"You're handling a prosecutor and a judge, how hard can a school be?"

"You'll want someone with experience in this kind of thing. If you want, I can recommend someone."

"I'll handle the school myself," Dad says.

I'm screwed.

Mom looks relieved, like she thinks he can stand up to Henderson or something. "You have nothing to worry about," she tells me. "Your father will fix everything for you. He was going to be a lawyer once, you know."

Yeah, but he was only good enough to become a mechanic. He'll enjoy the chance to play Lionel Hutz. He's been all over Patterson with advice and suggestions. I'm surprised the man hasn't told him to zip it.

"Getting the school to change their stance won't be easy, Celeste," Dad says.

Mom's head snaps around. "But it will be done. They have to let him return. You have to make them."

"The administration has concerns about student safety and considers Malik a danger. And I'm concerned that he was drunk."

"I was not drunk." I jump to my feet and throw my arms in the air. "I told you, two, maybe three beers max. It was a party. That's what people do at parties, they have fun and feel alive."

I glance at the lawyer and see he's staring at me.

Patterson looks both puzzled and sad. "You do understand there must be no more drinking. No alcohol at all. Can you do that?" He sounds like he's issuing a challenge.

"No problem. I'll be sober as a judge for the judge."

"This isn't funny. If you violate probation in any way, the deal will be history. That will leave your mother very unhappy."

"I'm already unhappy," Mom says. "This place is corrupting Malik. We should have left here long ago. I wanted out of the city but you," she points at Dad's chest, "you had to stay. If we had taken him away from this place and the horrible influences, that problem would have disappeared. But you want on the mayor's task force so much you'll stay here and sing its praises while your son is dragged down by bad influences. That's why he gets in trouble."

Yeah, Mom, blame Dad, the city, the world.

"He got in trouble because he was drinking," Dad says.

"The geographic cure seldom fixes real problems," the lawyer says. "If the problem is here, it needs to be faced here."

Mom whirls on him. "You don't understand our issues. Just get out there and deal with the court."

Mr. Patterson pushes back his chair and stands. He looks sad instead of angry. "I guess I'll take the geographic cure myself and depart. Dinner was excellent, Mrs. Kaplan."

After he leaves, I grab an energy drink from the fridge. It's the strongest thing in the house. Dad refuses to have liquor around, even for holidays or their anniversary. Mom sometimes has a glass of wine, but Dad only drinks battery acid disguised as coffee. If he would just toast life with a little *l'chaim* once in a while, he might understand the world better.

I open the can and drink deep. Dad approaches, walking with a slow, deliberate tread. He stops in the center of the kitchen. We stare at each other. Did I really think things would be different? That this time he'd be on my side? That he'd say, *Malik is my son. That's all that matters.*

A sudden rattling sound makes me start. I realize it's the refrigerator's motor kicking in. I finish my drink and toss the empty can in the garbage.

"Do you understand how badly you beat that boy?" Dad asks. "Do you even care?"

"Spencer needed a lesson."

Dad takes off his glasses and pinches his nose. His eyes lift to the ceiling like he's hoping God will finally pay attention and fix his unworthy son. "Is that all you're going to say? You may be my son, but you're not the boy I watched grow up. I don't even know you."

You never did.

CHAPTER 8

Why do you stay with me?" I asked Cesare in the days when our parents became enemies.

"You're my friend," he answered back then. "I won't abandon you."

Today, Cesare and I walk outside the school. Mr. Russo hurried back right after the arrest, so Cesare and I had to lay low for a few days, but he's back on the road again. Old Man Russo hates my dad and me and pretty much anything else that begins with the letter K. That includes knife—otherwise I'd worry every time he returns from a cross country run in his eighteen-wheeler.

It's evening, but lights still shine from some of the windows. The temperature can't be more than thirty degrees. Freezing wind smacks my cheeks. A light dusting of snow falls from heavy gray clouds. If I had my car, Cesare and I would be driving down Lake Shore Drive, watching winter waves pound the beach and blasting the MP3 player.

"How'd you make out?" Cesare asks.

"A fine, an essay, and community service at some place for the homeless." When Spencer came in to make his "victim statement," the judge looked at me like I was slime. Dad wouldn't look at me at all. I got everything the lawyer said. Probation, along with a hundred hours of community service. Restitution and the predicted fine. And let me not forget the freaking essay.

"An essay?" Cesare looks interested.

"Yup. I'm supposed to do five hundred words, like some grade-schooler." Five hundred words of "I'm sorry." Might as well be five million, because that will never happen.

"Do you even know five hundred words?" Cesare asks, and then ducks when I toss a punch at him. "How's it going?"

"Vandalism is bad. Fighting is worse." I laugh. "Four hundred ninety-four more words and I'm done."

"I could write it for you."

"No." That's not what I need from my friend.

"How's your dad taking things?"

I shrug. "I'm not worried, except he intends to sell my car to pay the fine. I'll do the dumb community service, but I have to save my ride."

"Not everyone gets to just sell a car to get what they need. Not everyone even gets to have a car." Cesare's tone is too sweet. Almost disrespectful.

"You sound like you think I should feel sorry for you."

"You have a wealthy old man to buy you everything, even a cushy community service gig. You're not hurting."

Total disrespect. I sacrificed myself for him, and he wants to throw that back in my face. Where's the gratitude? I'm the only reason he's still on the court.

*

On Saturday morning, I drag myself out of bed for my first day of court-ordered community service. There's another message from Nicole on my phone: *Call me. Now!!*

"You do not own me," I mutter, and delete the text. Nicole is pretty, and having her around makes guys envy me. But deep inside there's nothing to her, and I haven't been in the mood for a nothing moment since my arrest.

Maybe I'm sick.

I send a message to Cesare to set up a meeting this afternoon, after I finish my first stint at the shelter. Six impossible hours. *God, kill me now.* Mr. Patterson claimed Dad pulled in a lot of favors to get me this assignment. I should find that judge and tell him that forcing me to spend six hours of prime time in a homeless shelter every Saturday is no favor.

I shower, pull on a Chicago Bulls hoodie and jeans from the pile in front of the closet and head downstairs, following the sound of grease popping in a skillet and the smell of coffee.

When I enter the kitchen, Mom steps away from the stove and looks me over. I know what she's going to say before she opens her mouth. "Shouldn't you put on something neater? Dress up a bit? It's your first day on the job."

"This isn't a job; just a bunch of people who better be glad I show my face." I'll be among street people in rags; what will my clothes matter? The hoodie is clean. I've only worn it once this week. I lift an arm and sniff my pit to check. I followed Dad's instructions and dressed up for court, but I still got hammered.

"I want you to make a good impression. It would only take you a few minutes to change."

"No time. It's a long hike, and I'm on foot now, remember?" Maybe if I lay it on Mom, she'll go after Dad and get me my car back. I cram a piece of toast and ham into my mouth.

"At least put on a coat. It's cold."

My jacket and hoodie are all the protection I need. I don't surrender to cold. I pull up the hood and shove my hands deep into my pockets as I walk.

I pass a liquor store. I slow my pace. Three guys lean against a car at one end of the parking lot. The breeze carries the barking sound of their laughter. I take a deep breath and finger my wallet. I could probably get one of them to buy me a little something to make today bearable.

One guy hitches his pants and starts toward me. I shake my head and continue walking. My dry throat aches, but there's no telling what will happen when I get to my assignment. I can't chance having a bottle on me if I get searched, or risk having someone smell alcohol. No matter what some fools claim, even Vodka can be smelled on your breath. I know that from experience.

The large, gray brick three-story house I find looks a little like a warehouse. There's not even a sign out front letting the neighbors know who lives inside. It's bigger than Dad's McMansion. There are only a few windows, and shutters cover every one; they don't want anyone seeing what's inside. The windows are weather-stripped for the coming winter, and the paint looks fresh. A couple of bare-branched trees stand in the snow-covered yard.

I knock on the door. No one comes. Minutes pass and my anger grows. I'm on time; why aren't they ready for their court-ordered gopher? I look for a doorbell, but there isn't one—just a keypad attached to the door. It bears the logo of the same security company Dad uses for our house. It's the system I learned how to disable years ago.

I push the buzzer under the smooth plastic keypad. Seconds later, a woman's loud, angry voice comes through the speaker. "Can't you read? No solicitations means get lost; we're not buying anything."

Maybe that means I can leave and say they refused me.

No, that judge had no sense of humor.

"It's Malik Kaplan, and I'm supposed to be here," I yell.

Miss Mad-At-The-World makes me show my driver's license and doesn't apologize when she finally opens the door. She escorts me down a hall. Floorboards creak. I hear some kid crying behind one of the closed doors we pass. As we near the end of the hall, we walk past a kitchen where three women are cooking. I smell chicken and burgers and feel my stomach rumble. In the next room, I see two more women and a teenaged girl setting plates on a long wooden table. One woman looks up and scowls like I'm a monster.

I will not do kitchen duty. Not six hours a week with a house of women who consider me an enemy. Not even for that devil judge.

We reach a door labeled Constance Wiggins, Director.

The woman escorting me pushes open the door and shouts, "Connie, your designated slave has arrived."

CHAPTER 9

I expect some ancient lady, gray hair done in a beehive, glasses and age spots, probably in need of a hearing aid. One of the freaks who just barely chose saving the world over raising a houseful of cats. This lady looks younger than Mom. She wears an oversized Bears t-shirt as ratty as my sweatshirt. No wedding ring. She's not bad look-ing. She should dump the baggy duds and get into something young, head to a club where she can loosen up with a few drinks, make a hook-up, and start a real life.

Her desk overflows with stuff: A computer and printer, a cup holding pens and pencils, and a potted plant. A portable heater sits in a corner. There are two metal chairs in the room, one filled with books and the other with papers. Obviously she doesn't get a lot of visitors. Or else she likes making people stand around.

"You must be Malik, Dwayne Kaplan's son," she says when the other woman leaves, closing the door behind her. "I've been looking forward to meeting you. My name is Constance Wiggins."

"I got that already; I'm not blind." I move the books from one chair, place them on the floor, and flop down in the seat. The metal digs into my back. "How much did my dad pay you to take me?"

"Excuse me?" Connie almost jumps out of her seat.

"He gives you money, right?"

Her voice grows soft when she says, "If you're asking about dona-tions to the shelter, then yes, Dwayne Kaplan has been a godsend."

"I bet he has."

"Too many people believe the homeless deserve their problems, even in today's horrid economy. With all the state cutbacks, we would have had to close our doors long ago without your family's generous support."

"Thought so." I lean back in my chair, cross my ankles, and thrust my hands in my pockets. I wonder if she finds Dad more than just a generous wallet? She's young, pretty, and has no scars.

"If you think I've been paid to take you on, think again. You're here because the judge assigned you to me. I need help, as do the families forced to live here. If you don't feel you can do the job, I'll let you explain that to the judge. I won't keep a troublemaker."

Pipes clang as somewhere inside the building, someone turns on a faucet. "I'm guessing there's a lot to do around this place."

"There's always something that needs to be done." She massages her forehead—a slow, weary gesture. "Except for my office and the shared spaces—kitchen, laundry area, bathrooms on each floor, and a small play area in the basement—every inch of this building has been turned into family apartments. And still it's not enough. We're at capacity. Every room, even those needing repairs, is filled with mothers and their minor children. The mothers have it bad, the kids worse," she continues. "We can give them a roof, heat, and meals, but they still get to see hell at a very young age."

"Only mothers? What about men?" I ask.

Connie leans back in her chair and runs a hand over her face. "We only take mothers and their minor children at this location. Security is a major concern. We have a curfew, and residents must be inside the doors on time or they get locked out for the night. Too many violations, and..."

When she pauses, I run a finger across my throat and grin.

"It's not funny, especially with small children involved." Her voice rattles like an overheated engine.

"I get that, Connie."

"My name is Miss Wiggins."

"The other lady called you Connie."

"I'd prefer that *you* call me Miss Wiggins."

I'd prefer to be somewhere else. We just don't get what we want, do we? But I'm already beginning to respect Connie. I think of scared kids and a house full of women, and Connie having to tell one of them she has to leave. My guts squirm. If Dad hadn't agreed to marry Mom, would she and Perry have ended up in a place like this?

Mom was a fifteen-year-old sophomore. Her parents swore they would disown her when they found out she was pregnant. They're dead now. She says they wouldn't have really kicked her out on the streets, but I've met her brothers. If her father was anything like his sons, he meant his threat. In the end, those oh-so-devout Catholics forced Dad to marry her, only two days after he graduated. In their wedding pictures, Mom holds her flowers in front of her, obviously trying to hide her growing stomach.

I overheard Mom's brothers talking once. Statutory rape—only they claimed it wasn't all that "statutory." When Uncle Leon tried to stand up for Dad, they almost fought him. *I never forgave my old man for making Celeste marry him*, Mom's oldest brother said. *I don't care how much money Dwayne has now, I don't forgive him.*

I don't forgive him, either.

Connie's hand goes to her face again. This time she massages her eyes. "Resident and staff safety are paramount; that means residents are expelled when necessary. We had to let a few of the older boys go a few days ago after they repeatedly failed drug tests. Two of their mothers chose to leave with them. Sad, but…" Connie shrugs. "Our waiting list never goes down."

"Meaning you don't care who's in those rooms."

"I care, but there must be rules." Her voice grows brittle and she gives me the same hard-eyed scowl I saw on the judge's face. "You're still young enough to sneer, but rules serve a purpose. Ours ensure that residents are safe from abusive situations and economic distress. We give them training, confidence, a chance for a new start. We have classes in everything from computer skills to money management and homemaking. As a result, most of our residents eventually find jobs and places of their own. Our success rate is extremely high."

Her voice grows louder. Her eyes sparkle as she adds, "I love closing the doors on families making a new start."

"What's my role, Connie?"

The sparkle disappears. "Call me Miss Wiggins. You're going to be part of the staff, Mr. Kaplan. Act like it."

"After you and I square away our own rules. No dishes."

She blinks rapidly. "Excuse me?"

"What's my part in this operation? If you say dishwasher, I'm out of here. Same for washing clothes."

"Are you willing to explain that to the judge?"

"As long as he explains why cops waste time busting guys trying to have fun, when they should be going after murderers and robbers." Maybe that hardass judge should have just said "lock Kaplan up," because if *Miss Wiggins* tries handing me an apron, I'll march back to the cell and let Mom take it from there.

Connie steeples her hands and stares at me for a long time, almost like she's trying to see inside me. "I don't suppose someone like you has ever had to worry about your next meal."

She doesn't know, and I won't tell her. Maybe I never had to live in a shelter, but before the Kaplan family had "Six Chicagoland Locations," we had *nothing*. I was always the last kid picked up from kindergarten because my parents took all the overtime they could. I got sick once and tried to hide it, because sickness meant money and even at five, I knew we didn't have any. We had debts and payments and creditors. I went to bed hungry and dreamed of food and warmth and safety and other things I could not have. Then came Mom's accident and the insurance money that changed everything.

Suddenly we had enough; more than enough. Only I didn't believe the good times would last. I ate and stuffed and hoarded until I blew up to giant-sized while waiting for the return of emptiness. Mom gave me anything I wanted, Dad's lips tightened, Uncle Leon laughed, and Perry…my brother grew disgusted with me. He claimed I was too fat and soft to be his real brother, that I was barely even a real guy. Soon, every kid in my school repeated his words.

Now it's my turn to give back and shove other chumps around. Only it doesn't help. No matter what I do, not one memory fades.

"I'm good with machines," I tell Connie. "No lie. Give me any engine and I can fix it. Electrical, mechanical, even plumbing. That's the kind of work I can do for you. I just need something real."

She looks at her hands, but I see her shoulders shake with suppressed laughter. "What say we compromise? You help me help some kids not become murderers or robbers, and I make sure you don't have to deal with dirty dishes or clothes."

She waits until I nod.

"At the moment, we have three elementary school girls and one ten-year-old boy." She rises from her chair as she speaks. "He's very withdrawn. He has an older brother, but we couldn't allow Lamont in—he's nineteen, almost twenty. The separation has left the boy angry," she says, as she leads the way out of the office. "At his mother, me, the world. But we had no choice. Even if I could make an exception, it would not be for Lamont. He barely tried to hide his gang allegiance and drug use, and harassed staff and some of the older girls. Right now, the little boy pretty much hates everyone inside this building, especially me. But he doesn't know you."

"You want me to babysit an angry snot?"

She continues walking and talking, like she doesn't catch my sarcasm. "I understand you're an athletic hero."

"Hero," I mutter. Boy did she get suckered.

"Exactly." She sounds so enthusiastic I want to puke. "You can serve as a youthful role model who can show the boy the importance of school, and build up his self-esteem."

"I'm no role model. Make me a handyman and let one of your people take the kid on."

"The men on staff are older and handle night security and custodial issues. They wouldn't be right for this situation. I think you're the perfect age to reach this boy. You can be a big brother."

Cesare should have this gig. He knows how to be a big brother. I couldn't even handle the role of little brother.

Connie takes me down a set of stairs. "Like many of our kids, he had to transfer schools when he moved here. We keep students' stays here a secret. The school cooperates so the kids aren't teased, but transferring in the middle of a school year is still traumatic."

"You're kidding, right?"

She stops on the bottom step and stares at me with her lips pursed. "Can't you put yourself in someone else's place for even a minute?"

I meant the teasing thing. If you're different, if you're helpless, the guys with power always find out. Things can't have changed that much in the four years since I attended the local grade school. The badass living inside the house with me was scarier than anyone inside the school, but the teasing and bullying at school was still hell until Cesare and I teamed up. As for not knowing the new kid lived in a homeless shelter—even without a sign on the building, that kind of secret wouldn't last the first week.

We reach the basement. Connie barely slows as she bends to pick up a doll. To the left I see washing machines, dryers, and plumbing fixtures. On the right are bookshelves and tables. A few girls are bent over a table, giggling and writing. Beyond the library space is an even smaller recreation area where someone set up a sagging volleyball net. Wishful thinking—the ceiling is high, but not high enough to play. A boy sits on a basketball with his back to us and his head bent.

"There he is," Connie says.

"What do you expect me to do, help him get off the ball?"

Again she misses my sarcasm. "Keep him company. Tutor him; his schoolwork is suffering. Mostly, just be with him—show him the world isn't as bad as he thinks."

In other words, lie.

No problem.

I walk over and squat beside the kid. His gaze doesn't leave the floor.

"What are you staring at?" he asks through clenched teeth.

Someone who reminds me too much of myself.

He has short black hair. His skin is a smooth caramel. His shoulders are tensed up against his ears, and deep furrows cut through his forehead. He clutches a stuffed animal in his arms.

"Let me see." I hold out my hands. He shakes his head, so I insist, "Hand over your animal."

"It's not mine," he says and throws the thing at me.

"I know that. It's a fox." The red fur and big tail are a total giveaway. "Foxes are wild and free; they don't belong to anyone."

He nods. "Wild and free."

"Just like us." I reach into my pocket and pull out a package of chewing gum. I put one piece in my mouth and hand him another.

He takes the gum, but won't look at me. I hear his feet tapping on the floor.

"Wassup?" I ask.

The tapping sound stops. "Nothing. Go away." He scoots around to keep from having to see me, a tactic I remember using on Mom when I was his age. When I got mad at her I'd turn my back and pretend she had disappeared. What I really wanted back then was to be scooped up and hugged and told things would get better.

I'm not about to hug this kid, but I move so I can see his face. "What's your name?"

He blinks and looks at me like I'm brainless. "Didn't the wicked witch tell you I'm trouble?"

"The witch's name is Connie. What's yours?"

"T'Shawn."

"I'm Malik."

I extend my arm and we bump fists. And now I'm lost. I don't know what to do next.

I point to the ball he sits on. "What this place needs is a basketball hoop."

"Dumbo, the ceiling's not half high enough." He snorts and rolls his eyes.

I look around and pretend to consider his words. "You're right. I bet volleyball doesn't really work here either."

"It does the way the girls play."

I laugh and ask, "Did you play with your brother?"

T'Shawn's head snaps around. "Who said I had a brother?"

I point to Constance standing next to the girls.

"That old lady's got a big mouth," T'Shawn says.

"You think?" We both nod. I sit on the floor and he keeps his eyes on me. We chew our gum. His foot begins tapping again.

"I don't need you," he says.

"You know that and so do I, but how about you do a guy a favor and pretend you're getting something out of me being here, so I don't end up back in jail?"

His eyes widen and the tapping stops. "You been in jail?"

Jail fascinates everyone except my parents. I decide to let that one night in a cell count for something.

"I'm the baddest of the bad," I say. "Even cops step aside when they see me coming."

"Whoa." His eyes grow into circles.

"They have a sign over the corner cell with my name on it." I lift my hands like I'm writing in the air. "Reserved for Malik Kaplan."

"Double whoa."

CHAPTER 10

A reserved cell with your name on it? No way that kid believed you." My cousin, John Henley, pauses on the way downstairs to our granddad's garden apartment. John is a Henley, not a Kaplan, because Uncle Leon, Dad's older brother, enlisted in the army rather than marry John's mother.

John is twenty-three, a month younger than Perry would have been. They went to high school together and led the football team, Perry as quarterback and John as offensive tackle. John is seven inches shorter than me, and ten pounds heavier, most of it in his gut. He has a small apartment, and a truck older than he is. He cares for that truck like it's a favorite child. He's the most religious member of our family. He drove all the way to Tein Li Chow's Chinese take-out in Evanston to make sure Granddad's favorite meal, Mongolian beef with eggrolls, was kosher. The smell of the food makes my stomach grumble. It wants to get inside and eat. But my brain is okay with waiting.

You never see John without a *kipah* on his head, and he's at Temple Beth Shalom with many of Chicago's most devout Hebrew Israelites almost every Sabbath. He even got the hospital where he works as a nursing assistant to set up a schedule that lets him leave before sundown on Fridays. He also gets Yom Kippur, Rosh Hashanah, and most of Passover off. When he told me about his modified schedule, he laughed and said, "Probably just means I'm at the bottom of the ladder, so no one cares when I'm not at work."

I don't think so. I think he's something special. I bet the guys he works for think so too.

It's Monday, and after another day of no school, John picked me up and brought me with him. We go together because Waymon Kaplan is a lot for one guy to put up with. I did a better job choosing my grandfather than my father. Granddad and I cruise along the same speedway, while Dad remains stuck down in the pit.

All the way here, I've been telling John about the shelter.

"Swear to God, T'Shawn thinks I'm huge." I hold my arms wide.

"He's young and dumb, but even so—a reserved cell?"

"Don't pretend you don't remember being ten. He believed everything. The only time he stopped listening to me was when he bragged about his big brother. Lamont says this and Lamont says that. Apparently that dude's in lockup every other week." Something about the way T'Shawn's shoulders hunched when he said his brother's name made me wonder if he was as upset over Lamont's absence as he claimed.

"You want to go back and see that kid again, don't you?"

"I have to go back. Judge's order, remember?" I can't admit that I like the shelter, and the kid. By the time I left, T'Shawn was talking and moving with major swagger and a big-toothed grin. His strut reminded me of the days when I felt like hot stuff because Perry let me hang with him. When I was ten, I still thought I could gain his approval.

Granddad is sixty-five and lives alone in a garden apartment with only his radio, TV, and Internet connection to keep him company. He has the radio on when we arrive, tuned to a talk station, his personal favorite. He can't drive because of an old DUI. He lives on Social Security benefits and has no money for a good lawyer to fight the system holding him down. The father of the officer who arrested him was one of the neighborhood nerds back when Granddad ruled the streets. He made sure Granddad was targeted. Uncle Leon wants to help him get his license back, but he doesn't make much money. My dad has money, but refuses to help.

"Which of you is my favorite grandson?" Granddad says as he opens the door. He scratches his chest and leers.

"He is." John and I point at each other.

Our battles with Granddad are a family tradition. I'd happily leave the honor of being the favorite to John, but it's clear Granddad intends to take us both. John and I barely have time to get through the door before the old man begins throwing punches.

John accepts a quick hit to the stomach, groans, and says, "You got me." He falls against the wall with his hands covering his chest. Then he takes the food to the kitchen and begins filling plates. I prepare for my turn.

The old man throws a punch at my shoulder. I forget and block his fist. Then things really begin. His face tightens and the blows come faster until I remember to drop my guard and let him land a punch to my jaw. Letting him win is the only way to stop the game we've played my whole life. I watched Perry defeat him once. The old man wouldn't speak to my brother for months afterward.

"Keep your left high." Granddad grins with pride. "Doesn't that coach of yours teach you the need for defense? What is his name, anyway? Castle, King…"

"Kasili, and he doesn't teach me anything anymore, thanks to that judge." I rub my jaw and join John at the kitchen table. I grab a pair of chopsticks, hoping Granddad will understand that I don't feel like talking.

"They'll lose every stinking game without you." Granddad drops into his chair and drinks from a coffee cup. "Your father should never have let this happen; he should have fought for you. He had a duty to you. A man's first duty is to himself, but right after that comes family."

"And after that?" John asks.

"After that comes nothing. Take care of family, that's it."

"What about friends?" John's eyes narrow. "You know, the guys who watch your back?"

"Friends?" Granddad takes another drink. His movements are jerky, as if his joints ache more than usual. "When I was overseas on the enemy line, I didn't want friends; I wanted soldiers who respected the uniform, who said 'yes, sir,' saluted, and marched when sent out to face enemy fire. Friends give you that 'do I have to?' bullshit. So-called friends are just enemies wearing disguises, and you can't trust anyone who hides what he really is. You can trust a man who fears you because you always know what he'll do, understand?"

"Understood," I say, even though Granddad is wrong about friends. He doesn't get Cesare and me; he never thought our friendship would last. But it's easiest just to agree with him.

"See, that's why you're my favorite grandson." Granddad points his fork at me. "Once you get back in school, you'll show them all."

"*If* I get back. Dad's playing lawyer and 'discussing the situation' with the school." He went in to face the admin today. When I get home, he'll shrug and explain how I'll have to live with his failure and kiss Farrington goodbye.

I shouldn't care.

I hate knowing that I do.

"Uncle Dwayne is a good negotiator," John says. "You'll be okay."

"You mean because he talks people into paying inflated prices for repairs they don't need?" Granddad tears off a piece of eggroll, chews, and swallows. "Dwayne is a jellyfish. You should have played football, Malik. No football coach would ever let a star player be suspended."

"Football scrambles your brains," John says. "Perry got sacked so often—"

"You were on the line—it was your job to protect him." Granddad's voice is as rough as an unmuffled engine. He takes another drink from his coffee cup and burps. "If I'd had to deal with a line that let any two-bit player crash through, there'd have been hell to pay."

John's hand tightens around his fork. "If my jackass cousin had spent less time posing for pictures, maybe he'd have known the plays better."

"Don't talk about Perry like that."

John's lips press together. "I know. The dead can do no wrong."

In the extended silence, I hear a voice yelling from the radio: *Urban Management, that's another waste of taxpayer money. Giving to the cheating rich who are already robbing the poor, namely you and me.*

Impossibly, the speaker sounds angrier than the men in the room with me.

Granddad grunts. "Dwayne's another one of those cheaters."

"Don't blame Uncle Dwayne because people like to complain." John looks up, his eyes unreadable. "'Save me, give me, don't blame me.' Too many people want something for nothing."

"Why shouldn't a man get what's coming to him? I got nothing against businessmen. Hell, a man walks into a boardroom, he's got to face down his own set of enemies. But my son," Granddad pounds his chest as he speaks, "*my son* is a spineless coward who sits behind a desk in a back room and plots against his neighbors. There's nothing more despicable than a man who won't face you man-to-man." Granddad's fist slams on the table, shaking it. His coffee cup falls over.

I grab a towel from the sink and return to clean up the spill. As I suspected, there was more than coffee in that cup. The smell of alcohol wafts up from the towel.

"Dwayne seems to think these streets are his kingdom," Granddad continues. "He gobbles up everything in sight, taking over one foreclosure after another. He has some master plan, wants to own the entire city, I bet. He doesn't even have to fight for turf like a real man. His weapon is his wallet."

I surprise myself by saying, "Dad works hard. He makes good money."

"Why defend him? Oh, yeah, he's your old man. You have to." Granddad leans toward me as if confiding a big truth. "I could make good money too, if I were willing to cheat people. Look what he did to Russo, his so-called friend. Dwayne would have been better off without children. He only went after Celeste because Leon wanted her. My poor boy fell apart after he watched the girl he loved with his brother. That's how Paula caught him on the rebound."

When Granddad mentions John's mother, a muscle jerks in John's cheek. He can't stand his father. Most people love Leon Kaplan. Except Mom. She may have liked him once, but that's long gone. She and Paula Henley are now best gossip buddies and join with John as members of the We-Hate-Leon-Kaplan club.

John tosses down his fork and says, "I have to go. Mom needs me to help her with something this afternoon."

"Something?" Granddad's tone calls John a liar.

My cousin leaves the room. I follow and lean against the front door to keep him from opening it and abandoning me.

"You can't leave me here," I say in a low voice. "We were supposed to do this together."

"Come with me. I can't stay any longer. A little of that old man goes a long, long way."

John glances back into the kitchen and lowers his voice. "We're not the world's friendliest family. Watch out for that chin of yours. Learn how to give in."

"I let the old man win."

"Not soon enough. Some fights aren't worth it, little cousin."

"I'm not little."

"That's what makes you a target." John gives a soft chuckle before stepping through the door. I listen to him go up the stairs until I hear him exit the building. Then I close the door and lean against it until my heartbeat slows and I'm ready to face my granddad again.

"I'm glad it's just us," the old man says. He goes to the fridge and pulls out two cans of beer. He sets one in front of me.

"You know I'm on probation," I remind him. "Dad's lawyer says I shouldn't." My heart beats faster and my chest grows tight as I look at the beer and anticipate the coming buzz. Perry handed me my first beer when I was ten. When I drank it, I suddenly felt truly human. Superhuman even. I stopped being afraid of anything. Even him.

"Dwayne has no respect for you; he treats you like a child. I say you're a man. And you're in my place, so no one will know but us. Drink." He settles back in his chair. I hear the cracking sound as he opens his own can. "Dwayne is all soft on the outside and softer still at the core. I'm surprised he had the stones to produce a man like you. Thank God you're like me—no one scares you."

He does.

I drink my beer so I don't have to speak.

CHAPTER 11

Granddad doesn't fall asleep until after we run out of beer. It's dark when I pull on my M65 field jacket and leave his apartment. The green camo material settles over my shoulders like a suit of armor. No John means no truck to take me home. I consider catching a bus. Then I begin walking.

Christmas lights hang from trees and shine in windows, telling the lie that all is right with the world. But not with my life. I had just enough beer for a buzz, not enough to drown my worries. What will I do without school? My friends and I complain about school all the time, but this is my senior year.

I've gone two blocks down near-empty streets when I see a girl walking a half-block ahead of me on the other side of the street. Even though she's bundled up in a scarf, boots, and long winter coat, I know who she is.

Barney.

My skin heats up the way it never does around Nicole.

She slows and stiffens, almost like she feels me staring. She stops. Looks around. Our eyes meet through a gap in the traffic separating us. Barney scowls like she sees her worst enemy. I know what people are saying about me; I've followed the tweets since my arrest. The stories grow more impossible every day. They say I robbed a bank, killed the Schrumms in their sleep, and even planned to blow up the school. I wonder how much Barney believes. She knows what I'm like. After all, we dated for two weeks before I stole her diary and blackmailed her.

I like having people fear me. Life is safer that way. You never have to duck your head or pretend to be invisible, not when you're on top. I also liked Barney the superwoman, the girl who was ready to stand up to me, to beat me up, or at least to try. It was crazy. A freshman girl ready to take on me, Cesare, and another member of my posse, over some skinny geek she barely knew. She balled up her fists and jumped in to defend him. I was so surprised, I almost bit my tongue to keep from laughing. I felt drawn to her all over again. I wanted her on my side, not against me.

But I don't like the look I see in Barney's eyes now.

She starts walking again. Her long legs cover ground quickly. Too quickly. I see a man in front of her only a second before she halts to avoid bumping into him. He stands near an alley entrance, just outside the light cast by the streetlamp. The guy is a squat human mountain in dreadlocks that hang around his shoulders. Barney is taller than he is. He won't like having to look up at a girl. I don't need to see colors or a tattoo to know Dreadlocks is another Enforcer.

Barney starts to walk around him. He moves to block her path. He says something. Barney foolishly shakes her head no.

I look around, wondering if anyone else sees this. Cars rush by, moving fast like the drivers don't want to spend an extra second in this area. No people, either; just the three of us walk on this block. There's good and bad in that. The bad: no witnesses to give him second thoughts about whatever he's planning. The good: there's no sign of any other gang members.

That's actually a major plus. Enforcers need numbers to enjoy that we-are-God feeling and whatever-we-want-we-take kind of power. Dreadlocks is alone. If Barney gives him the proper respect, that will end things. He'll give her some smack talk and then let her pass.

Barney tries to walk around him again. He blocks her again, and reaches for the purse hanging over her shoulder. The rainbow colored bag is practically big enough to hold a house.

Be smart—let him have it.

She slaps his hand away.

"Stupid," I mutter. I give her props for bravery, but that move cost her big points. There's a time to fight and a time to let them take what they want so you don't get hurt.

It's not my business, I tell myself. *She's nothing to me except an enemy.* But

I'm already rushing into the street, dodging between a Chevy and a truck that almost clips my heels. Horns blare.

Barney hits the guy. Her fist might have stopped one of her skinny friends at school. But this behemoth grabs her arm, spins her around, and drags her into the alley. She yells once, her voice filled with frustration and anger. Then silence. They vanish as I blink.

I reach the curb and run into the shadows after them. The slush-laden alley is filled with debris: broken furniture, newspapers, and fermenting garbage. A cat yowls in the distance. A broken doll's head stares up at me from the ground. Dreadlocks has Barney pressed against a brick wall. One hand covers her mouth. She claws at his arms and her legs kick.

"Let her go." I stop, barely spitting distance away from them. Barney's eyes widen like she sees some kind of miracle.

Dreadlocks turns. "Does she belong to you?" His lips twist into something that might pass as a smile among his friends.

Salty sweat burns my chapped lips. I push back a sudden snakes-in-the-stomach feeling. I'm alone, no weapon, no Cesare, and obviously no freaking sense. I want to say she means nothing to me, but the words stick in my throat. Instead, I widen my stance into my fiercest pose, hands on my hips, head thrown forward as I toss out my brother's favorite threat. "You don't want to fuck with me, shithead."

Dreadlocks throws Barney to the side. She drops like groceries tumbling from a torn shopping bag. He cracks his neck and grins before advancing toward me.

"On the streets you have nothing," John told me once. *"It's not like being in the ring with rules, referees, forbidden punches, timeouts, and the good old ten-count. No gloves, no mat, and no corners. In a street fight, obey rule number one: run if you can. If you can't, get in the first blow, because he who hits first usually wins."*

My first blow is an uppercut. A crack sounds in the cold air, the impact shivering up my arm as his head snaps back. I bend, move in close, and get in a second blow. He stumbles and steps backward.

I've boxed before, in a ring, facing trained fighters. I start to relax. I'll put this dude down in no time. With Barney as a witness, this fight will provide a major boost to my rep.

Then Deadlocks pulls a knife.

CHAPTER 12

The knife changes everything.

This isn't a fight anymore. It's combat, and only one side has a weapon.

Dreadlocks is out to kill.

Screw pride, screw anger, screw everything except survival. I grab Barney's hand and yank her to her feet. We start to run, but she's limping. I don't have to turn to know how fast he's closing on us. We get maybe four steps and she falls.

Time slows.

Two choices flash through my head. Leave the girl and run like hell. Or turn to face him, knowing there will be blood.

Most of it mine.

I turn and step forward. I have time to yell, "Barney, run," before he lunges at me. I jump to the side, evading the gleaming blade.

"You the one needs to run." He laughs like a pirate about to poke his enemy in the ass with a sword and send him tumbling over the plank. "Last chance to come out of this alive."

I see the lie in his eyes. If I try to escape, I'll only get steel in my back. He swings the knife in a wide arc that catches the edge of my jacket. I move forward and block him with one arm, then throw a jab at his jaw with the other. It's a glancing blow. He grunts, steps out of my block, and slashes at me again.

The knife disappears into the folds of my jacket. I feel the material jerk, hear it rip; I feel a dull sting as the cold metal edge rips into my skin. Death's cold fingers tighten around my bones.

Focus. Stay alive. Give Barney time to get out.

He pulls back for another blow. I drop low and dive into the snow. Wetness seeps through my clothes as my slide brings me under him. I grab his leg, reach up and throw an elbow into the back of his knee while I jerk his foot. He falls. His heavy body lands on my chest. Fingers close around my throat. His other hand lifts the knife.

"Next time, mind your own damned business, hero," he growls, his stare ferocious and all-seeing. "Only you don't get a next time."

I kick and struggle, but I can't dislodge him. The knife descends.

I'm going to die.

My life does not flash before my eyes. All I see is the blade, already stained with my blood.

The lid of a garbage can hits his arm. The clang as the metal hits the knife echoes through the cold air. From the corner of my eye I see Barney on the attack. The knife falls from his hand. It flies through the air, whirls, and disappears into the dark. He jumps off me to go after Barney. He rips the lid from her and backhands her. There's a sickening sound of flesh on flesh and her quick scream before she goes down again.

I scramble to my feet and grab a soggy chair leg from the ground. The feel of wood in my hand brings me confidence. I hit him square in the back. I swing again before he can turn. He roars, releases Barney, and turns toward me, in time to receive another blow in the chest. He staggers back. I hit him again. He falls to all fours, coughing. His face twists with pain.

His head becomes my target. I remember everyone who ever had me backed in a corner in the days when I was young and helpless. I lift my weapon again. I can end it all here and now. I take aim. He'll never hurt me again.

"Malik, don't. He's already down," Barney calls out, before I can swing at his skull. She sounds like she's pleading. Like she's scared of what I might do next.

I step back. He looks from me to Barney. I have the only weapon now, and with Barney at my side, I have the odds.

"What next?" he asks, his voice shaky and filled with rage.

"You become a missing person," I say. "Now, before I change my mind."

He rises to his feet. Shadows hide his eyes, but not the blood leaking from his nose and mouth. He bends, reaching for his knife.

"No."

His hand stills. "But I need—"

"You need to go." Does he think I'm an idiot? "The knife stays here." I lift the chair leg and take a step toward him.

He jumps back and runs off, his footsteps fading as he blends into the darker shadows in the alley and disappears.

Barney grabs my chest. "Did he stab you? Are you hurt?"

"I'm okay," I say.

She unzips my jacket and runs her hands over the front of my sweatshirt like she's searching for something. The feel of her hands makes it suddenly hard to breathe and impossible to think.

"Adrenaline," she mutters. "That's it, you must be high on adrenaline."

"I'm not high on anything."

She takes a step backward. Her leg wobbles and she almost falls. I drop the chair leg and grasp her arm to steady her. She's soft and tough all at the same time. I feel strength in her muscles.

"Thank God you came," she says.

"Don't get mushy on me now." My side burns hotter with every breath. "Let's haul ass out of here." Barney and I better roll before Dreadlocks returns with reinforcements.

"My purse." Barney limps back to the wall.

"We don't have forever." I grab her purse, pick up the knife and shove it deep in my pocket, and take her arm. Seconds later, we are out of the alley and onto the sidewalk. I see one old man who gives us a quick look and then shrugs and keeps walking, not curious enough to ask questions.

We run to the end of the block and stand under the streetlight. We're both wet and smelly. I wonder what my face looks like. The wind picks up. I know how fear smells, all sweaty and sour. Right now there's no sign of that smell coming from Barney. Just the perfume that reminds me that she and I did have a few good times. Strands of black hair pull free from her braid and fly across her face. A bruise is growing on Barney's neck, and her shoulder seems stiff. I should have ignored her and hit the guy one more time.

"You can go now," she says. "Drive yourself home."

"I don't have a car. I'd take you home if I did."

"Is your car in the shop?"

"It's for sale."

"But you love that car." Her voice shakes. She sounds like she really understands. Like my loss matters to her.

The ground shakes as a bus approaches. It halts in front of us. We climb on board. While Barney fumbles in her bottomless purse, I pay both our fares.

"You didn't have to do that," she says.

"I know."

The engine growls; the bus lurches into motion. There are only three other people on it. We take seats near the front so she doesn't have to walk down the narrow aisle. The metal seats are hard. Barney is soft. What would she say if I put my arm around her?

I finger my side where the knife got me. Now that I'm sitting, the adrenaline she talked about begins to fade and my side burns. The knife didn't go deep and the wound feels like it has clotted shut, so I guess I won't bleed to death. I'm wet with blood and alley slush. I wonder if beer sterilizes from the inside. Crazy to go through all this and then die from some stupid infection.

Barney swallows and winces. "I can still feel his scratchy fingers digging into my throat."

"Why didn't you listen to me when I told you to run?" I ask.

"I couldn't leave you. How could I live with myself if I ran off while he hurt you? Or if I had to go to your funeral?"

Would she really have come to my funeral? I shake off that thought and say, "I don't know what things were like where you used to live, but you're here now. Life-In-The-Hood lesson number one: don't walk around alone after dark. Have a buddy. Better still, take the bus. Why be out on the street alone?"

She stiffens. "I just got off work."

"Work?" I almost forgot she has a part-time job as a waitress at Frank's Place, a restaurant near Granddad's apartment.

"You know, that thing most people do because their family can't toss them money. I missed a bus and I didn't want to wait for the next one. They're so far apart this time of night." She looks around and laughs. "I guess I might as well have waited."

"Why didn't you just give him your purse?" I thought all girls knew the trick. Open the purse, spill the insides on the ground, and then run like hell while your attacker goes after your stuff. It usually works when there's just one guy.

"I have my pay in my purse. Besides, that wasn't all he wanted." She draws herself up tight, a move that makes me swallow. "I've seen him before. He and some other guys came in the restaurant the other day, pretending they wanted to eat and hassling me. Frank pulled out one of his carving knives and did his 'I'm a veteran and I gutted my share of Taliban routine,' so they left. Next time I'll be ready. Yolanda has pepper spray; I'll get some from her."

"Which will just piss him off." I ignore the reference to my former girlfriend. Barney and Yolanda Dare became besties after Barney's brother stole Yolanda from me. "You do not want a pissed-off gangbanger after you. Life-In-The-Hood lesson number two: never mess with an Enforcer."

"If he doesn't mess with me, I won't bother him."

"That's not what I said, and you just failed the lesson."

The bus stops and another passenger boards. I put my arm around the back of the seat, ignoring the way the move jerks at my wound, and let my fingers rest on Barney's shoulder. I feel a spark as the past jumps up around me and my head aches with impossible thoughts. What if I had a time machine and could go back, back to that first day, before I handed her reasons to hate me?

I can't look away from her face, her hair. It's really her hair too, not like the hair extensions Nicole wears. But for some reason, Barney hates her hair. I know because I stole her diary. I wanted to know what she thought of me. I should never have read it—I knew that right away. But once her diary was in my hands, I had to open it. And once I started reading, I couldn't stop. She wrote how much she liked me. But there was more. About herself and about finding her mother's dead body.

If I still had my mother, I'd tell her everything. I need her. She was there for me every time I messed up.

I should have gone to Barney right then and let her know I understood. I could have shown her the scar on my neck, the one Perry gave me when I was ten and didn't get out of his way fast enough. Or the bloody collar I found hidden in his room a month after Cesare and I gave up searching for my lost terrier. Maybe I could have told her about Perry's death.

No. That only comes out in nightmares.

Barney draws in a deep breath. Is she thinking about me? Maybe remembering, the way I am? Wishing things were different?

"Barney…" I hesitate, not sure what to say.

"Shania told me what really happened." Barney sighs. "I'm sorry. I saw you standing over her and assumed you were bullying her."

"Assuming makes an ass of you…" Her sudden smile dries up the rest of my words.

"And me, yeah, I know." She swallows. "I really *am* sorry."

"No problem," I say. Not as long as she keeps smiling.

"You're not as bad as you pretend to be."

"I'm so bad I even scared the cops who arrested me."

"That's nothing to boast about." Barney bites her lower lip. "What was it like, living inside a cell?"

"It was only one night." Her question surprises me. She never seemed like a jail groupie or the type who likes a touch of gangster in a man. I turn my answer into a joke. "I didn't live there, just stopped by for a quick visit and said hello to my buds the cops. It was all fun and games, mug shots, fingerprints, the works. There was a smoking hot female cop rubbing her fine self all over me. I'd let her cuff me anytime. Why do you care? Planning any major felonies? Or has Saint David found his way inside a cell?"

She shivers. "You'd like that, wouldn't you?"

"That's perfect. David and I finally have something to share."

"You have nothing in common with my brother. I was just curious."

"Curiosity kills, shorty."

"I know," she says, her voice so soft I barely catch the words. "You were a hero tonight. When I tell people what you did for me—"

"Don't. Don't tell anybody anything."

"Why not?" Her brow wrinkles in confusion. Somehow that makes her look prettier. "Why are you okay with everyone knowing when you get in trouble, but not when you do something good? Afraid someone might actually start liking you?"

"Maybe I don't want people to like me." *Shit. Why'd I say that? Laugh. Make it a joke.* "Except the fine shorties, of course."

"Bull." She stares straight ahead, remaining silent until the bus approaches her stop. She rises and heads for the exit. When I get up too, she says, "You don't have to come any farther. I get it. You don't want people to know you wasted time on me."

"I came this far; I'll see you to your door." I keep following her off the bus and down the sidewalk to the house she and her family rent.

She stops when we reach the front door. "I want to say thank you." She stares down at the sidewalk as she speaks.

A sour-voiced "thank you," that we both know she doesn't mean.

My guts churn. Next she'll go inside, shut the door, and forget all about me. The truth is, she doesn't want her family to see us together. I can tell by the way she won't look at me. I want some emotion from her. Something, anything—even anger.

I always know how to make people angry. It's as easy as breathing.

I hitch my thumbs into my belt and lean in toward her and give a quick hip thrust before saying, "You know how you can repay me."

Her head snaps up. "You're smart enough to know that's never going to happen. I really thought you were being a good guy, but none of this was really about me, was it? It was all about who rules the streets. You were two pit bulls snarling over the same burial plot for your bone, but the bone itself didn't matter. When I first moved here, I thought, 'Great. It's a new start; I'll leave the past behind.' I even thought, 'Wow, there's a great guy, and he likes me.' Only you didn't, not really."

The first time I saw Barney, my head said "Wow," too. She had looks, a body—if she had brains too, I thought, she would be perfect. In the end, she had brains enough to push me aside.

"I can't understand how I could ever have…" She pauses.

"Could have what?"

Her breath hitches. "Could have ever crushed so hard on someone like you."

And now, after everything she went through dry-eyed, I see tears in her eyes. I thrust my fists into my pockets to keep from reaching out to hug her.

The perfect girl lifts her head high and walks through the door.

CHAPTER 13

God, John, you evil sadist!" I nearly take out my tongue biting back a yell as he digs at my side.

My jacket and shirt lie draped over the back of a chair in John's kitchen. He lives in a first floor, one-bedroom apartment. His possessions are scattered around the place. I wonder if he tells his girlfriends the same thing I tell Mom—that my room is a museum and my things are just on display.

After I left Barney, I hoofed it to his apartment. He started grumbling the second I knocked on his door. I had to fight to keep him from dragging me to an emergency room. I don't need doctors or a call home just so Dad can give me another look of disgust.

John is the only person who would understand. He used to be an Enforcer. When he gets upset, like now, his blood pounds, and the outlines of the old tattoos he had removed flare red on his light brown skin. Scars left from the beat-down he faced when he left the gang disfigure his back. I've heard that some gangs let people go pretty easy. In others the only way out is death. Enforcers take the middle ground. If you are still standing at the end of a beat-down, you are out. If you're crippled or brain-damaged, you're out. If you're dead, you're out *and* your former buddies show up for the funeral. A beat-down is meant to make you wish you had never chosen to leave, and to keep others from even thinking about it.

John faced six men, all hard-bodies, chosen by his leader. They were armed with anything and everything except the instantly lethal knife or gun. John had only his hands. As soon as he put down one guy, his newer, fresher opponent stepped up. Guys who had been John's friends laid bets on how long he would remain on his feet. No one collected. No one bet that he would last to the end. He even walked away on his own. Then he spent days in the hospital. John said it was worth it to be done.

While he recovered, Uncle Leon actually played like a real dad. He sobered up and stayed by John's side until he was released from the hospital. After that, John worked odd jobs while attending Harold Washington College, a community college in downtown Chicago, to become a CNA, a Certified Nursing Assistant.

"You need to see a real doctor." He pours peroxide on my cut as he speaks. Blood forms thick bubbles on my skin.

I suck in a deep breath and grit my teeth against the sting. He's not gentle, but that's because worry makes him heavy-handed. When I can speak again, I say, "I came to you; you're the damned nurse."

"Nursing assistant," he says in a hollow voice, like it's no big deal. He pulls a handful of gauze from his first aid kit and wipes up the bloody froth. Then he tosses the red-stained gauze into the growing pile in the garbage. "A hospital could reduce the scarring."

"Girls like scars. Besides, I don't come close to matching your collection."

"You might need a tetanus shot."

"I've had one." Thanks to a cut from a jagged piece of glass, I had a shot when I was ten. I remember hearing Mom scream at Dad about moving to escape the bullies while the emergency room doctor gave me the shot. I never told her the bully responsible sat at the dinner table with us and slept in the bedroom across the hall from mine.

"At least this isn't too deep. You're lucky. I assume you'll go to temple and pray. Or will it be Mass and a candle?"

"My jacket caught the knife; no divine intervention was required." I shiver hard—the adrenaline rush has totally worn off. I would have shed more than a few drops if the heavy folds hadn't caught part of the blow. The blade is almost as long as my hand.

John reaches for the blade. I pull it back. "Mine now."

"Yes sir, General Badass." He salutes and almost hits his own head. Then he frowns. "Who'll hold that spot in school if you don't get back?"

"Why do I care?" Spencer maybe. Whoever it is, he'll find out being a badass only looks like fun.

"Toss the knife, and set the jacket up on a pagan altar. Just don't ever let this happen again. What have I always told you about knife fights?" John asks.

"A guy can't let himself be pushed around. There's no respect in running," I mutter.

"There's no respect in dying. Only a crazy fights when he doesn't have to and can't win. When a guy comes at you with a knife, he doesn't want your respect and he doesn't want to fight. He's out to kill. You see a knife, you run away."

"I wanted to run. But I had to fight. There was a girl."

"And you had to show off."

I remain silent as he washes his hands and then pulls out a piece of fabric, scissors, and. . .

"Superglue?" I ask. "Are you going to glue me together?"

"Would you rather I used a needle? This isn't glue, it's Dermabond, and it will hold your skin together while it heals. Added value—it inhibits bacteria and will fall off all by itself in a few days."

"But it's glue." I feel like some first grader's art project as he cuts the material into thin strips, then uses the superglue, Dermabond, whatever, to attach each strip of material to one side of the cut. He pulls the sides of the cut together with the strips and glues them to the other side.

"General Badass, defeating the bad guy and showing off for your girlfriend," he says as he works.

"She's not my girlfriend, just someone from school."

"What's her name?"

"Doesn't matter, she hates me."

"She hates me." He smirks. "A memorable name, anyway."

"It's Barney."

"Barney. Still unusual for a girl."

"Her name is Barnetta, okay?"

"And she's smart enough to hate you. Sounds like a keeper."

"She's not my type." I say the words. I want to mean them.

"Those are the kinds of girls that grab us."

John finishes up by wrapping me in gauze. The cut and the cloth holding me together are hidden under the wrapping. He insists on driving me home so I don't miss curfew, and because he feels guilty.

"I shouldn't have left you at Grandad's. You wouldn't have been out on the streets if I had stayed and taken you home."

I wouldn't have been there. But Barney would have. She and Dreadlocks.

I go home and sleep. For the first time in ages, there's no nightmare about Perry. Barney fills my night. She smiles at me and shows her gratitude with more than just that pitiful "thank you."

A lot more.

CHAPTER 14

Two days later it's official. I'm returning to Farrington. I don't know whether to laugh or bury my head under the covers. I guess laying it on thick, which works so well on customers, also swayed the principal. I should have known; if Dad could keep Mom's family from skinning him alive, he could manipulate the school admin. Henderson must be bugging.

It's Wednesday, eleven days after Spencer's party, less than two weeks before winter break begins. Last night, Dad chanted an extra prayer after he lit the final candle for the last day of Chanukah. I think he wanted me to consider the news a kind of Chanukah *gelt*. I liked things better in the old days, when my parents gave out real *gelt*— chocolate coins wrapped in gold paper. Those were presents worth having.

I check my side. No redness and no pain. I had to toss the bloody shirt so Mom wouldn't find it, but I'm keeping the jacket forever.

I decide to wear a khaki army fatigue shirt with corporal chevron stripes on the right shoulder, black cargo pants, and black lace-up Stormtrooper boots. I hang a set of imitation dog tags around my neck before pulling on the jacket. I had thought about scanning eBay for an imitation prison jumpsuit. But the school colors are orange and black; someone might mistake my prison getup for school spirit.

The guard snaps to attention when I approach the metal detector at the school entrance. Four years in this place, and they still expect to catch me with contraband.

"Miss me?" I ask, as I walk through the machine.

"Like I miss my ex," he growls, sounding disappointed when the alarm remains silent.

It's good to be back. I almost wish I could have given the guy a thrill, but I ended up leaving the knife with John.

I'm early. First period won't start for another fifteen minutes. The halls are filled with signs of the season. Peace, love, and alleged joy to the world. Christmas trees, Kwanzaa kinaras and Chanukah chanikiahs fight for space with snowflakes and candles. I see a green-skinned Grinch on the wall outside the school office. Guess even Vice Principal Henderson has a sense of humor. The walls also contain signs telling us to have a happy and fun holiday, with messages about no sex or drinking—do they want us to be happy or not?—and encouraging school spirit.

Guys shuffle to the side as I pass. I know what people are saying about me. I've seen the tweets, the notes on SocialEase, the posts on student blogs. Some say I tried to kill the Shrumms in their beds, that I planned to bomb the school, or rob a bank.

I look around the hall, giving each girl a few seconds of attention. They smile. One touches her hair and licks her lips. Another leans close and whispers, "Did you hear about last night's game?"

"What was the score?"

"Seventy to sixty-nine."

"We lost by one point?" I knew the team couldn't stay lucky and keep winning without me. Coach Kasili must be salivating over my return.

She shakes her head. "Jules lobbed a last second three-pointer and we won."

"Oh. Well, good. That's great." So Julian Morales, who became acting captain while I was suspended, got to be the hero again. That ends once I resume my role. I don't understand why Cesare let that happen. He's a senior; he should have held the title until my return.

I hear rapid footsteps in the hall. "What's going on here?" Vice Principal Henderson's voice booms. He looks at me and grins like a cat that's waiting for the mouse trapped under its paws to cease kicking. He stops only a few feet away from me, so close I smell sweat and stale cologne and hear him wheeze.

"Yo, old man, you here to welcome me back?" I say.

"I've been looking for you, Malik." Henderson spits my name like it burns his tongue.

I eye the two men standing behind Henderson: one of the school custodians and a police officer in full gear—batons, cuffs, and a gun hanging from his belt. There's also a police dog.

"Hey boy," I say, thinking about Beastly, my old terrier. He was so fierce and protective he thought he was a badass Rottweiler. He even growled and snapped at my brother. The police dog—a black, hairy animal with a thick tail and pointed ears—isn't interested in me.

He is also a she.

"Let's go," Henderson says.

"Where?" I ask.

"Your locker."

When we get to my locker, the officer walks the police dog back and forth in front of it. She yawns, totally uninterested. The officer turns to Henderson and shrugs, saying, "It appears to be clean."

I lean against the wall and smile. "If you'd told me you planned a party for my return, I would have brought a little something to make your day."

Henderson is just screwing with my head. He can't think I'm fool enough to load my locker with drugs, especially not on my first day back. Even the custodian lifts his hand to hide a smile.

I step forward to work the combination, but Henderson points a finger at the custodian. "Break it open."

The custodian looks at me with a mournful shrug and pulls out a set of bolt cutters. The sound of breaking metal echoes in the hall. My lock falls to the floor in pieces.

"My dog says there's nothing here," the officer says after everything lies scattered in the hall. The dog sits and scratches behind one ear.

"I don't care." Henderson steps toward me, fist raised above his head. I don't move. The dog growls. The cop stiffens. The vice principal takes a deep, shuddering breath, glances at the officer, and lowers his hand. "You are dangerous. We had to let you back. But you have to obey my rules. Rule number one, stay away from Spencer Shrumm. You will not be in the same room with him for any reason. If you see him in the hallway you'd better turn and run—"

"I never run."

"Start." He bares his teeth as he growls out the words.

"What about lunch? We have the same lunch period."

"Be prepared to starve. Because if the Shrumm boy says you so much as brush against his shoulder, you're done. If anything happens to him, in a bathroom, or the gym, or anywhere inside this building or on these grounds, it will be on your head. Do you understand me?"

"Yeah." I cross my arms over my chest. "You're telling me when I finally go off on him, I get to be as bad as I want. Thanks for the tip."

"This isn't funny. I voted for your expulsion. If things were up to me—"

"It's a good thing nothing much is up to you," I say.

His nostrils flare so wide I expect to see dragon flames. He reaches his hand toward me.

"Do. Not. Touch. Me." I make my voice low and deep, imitating Uncle Leon, who learned a lot about intimidation during Operation Savage Shield, a jungle battle almost no one remembers and he can't forget. His war-is-hell expression is easy to copy.

Henderson's hand hangs in the air. I hold the stare until his eyes drop. He turns to the cop and custodian and tells them to go.

"Wait," I say as they walk away. "Don't you need to trash my varsity locker too?"

Henderson laughs like a playground bully. "You no longer have a varsity locker."

"What are you talking about?"

"I mean you are no longer a member of Farrington's team."

"You can't take me off the team."

"Don't you read the student code?"

Never.

"The code says extracurricular activities are a privilege. One you no longer deserve."

"The felony charge was dismissed."

"Doesn't matter." Henderson takes a step closer to me. "As long as I consider you a danger to our players and to other teams, I'm within my rights to remove you. Effective immediately." He whistles as he walks away.

I kneel to grab my things and toss them back into my locker.

When I slam the locker door, it clangs and bounces back open again. Life will suck until I get a new lock.

Who am I kidding? Life sucks right now.

CHAPTER 15

Nicole and Giselle are arguing in the open area of the school Commons at the beginning of fifth period. School spirit isn't all that's popping out of Nicole's winter-defying blue-and-white halter top. She looks up and sees me. Something about the way she stares makes me shiver. I wish she would come running over and throw herself at me. Wish she would put her arms around me and say, "No problem, Malik. Still you and me, no matter what." But she just turns back to Giselle.

"Maybe I don't need a man to do things for me," I hear Giselle say as I approach. She wears no makeup. Her nails are chewed short. She wears a bulky red sweater and black pants, and looks lost beside her sister.

"Maybe you're brain dead." Nicole flips her hair back. "You've got the looks to get anyone if you work it. Why waste yourself on a boy with no money and less class? If that fool dropped off the planet tomorrow he wouldn't be missed."

"I'd miss him," Giselle says. "I just want him out from under Malik's control. He can't say no to that guy." Her voice grows deep as she adds, "'Yo, Cesare, run into that fire and see how long it takes you to burn to a crisp.'"

She's trying to mimic *me*!

"It can't be that bad," Nicole says.

"It's worse, you just don't know. I love the guy, but I don't understand the hold Malik has over him."

"I don't keep Cesare chained," I say. "He's free to do whatever he wants."

Giselle jumps and turns. When she sees me, she wraps her arms around herself tightly, as if struggling to keep herself from doing something she would regret afterwards. She brushes past me, half running by the time she exits the Commons.

"What about me? What if I disappeared down a dark alley?" I put my arm around Nicole's shoulders as I speak. She feels rigid. It's like I'm holding one of the heavy bags at the Community Center gym.

"Sometimes I wonder if you have." Nicole pulls free. "I've been trying to reach you for days. Why didn't you return any of my calls or texts?" Her eyes narrow and her voice has an edge.

"I was busy."

"Too busy to text?"

Too busy to care.

Nicole pouts—not her best look. "What happened Monday night?"

"Nothing."

"Nothing? Then the Barn-girl lied about you two? You weren't out chasing extra-large babies?"

Oh hell. Barney talked.

Spencer hobbles through the Commons on his way to the cafeteria, leaning on a cane. He's surrounded by girls who apparently think he's a wounded celebrity. His legs worked perfectly when he showed up for my sentencing and gave the judge his "victim statement."

"What's up with you?" I point at the cane.

"You tried to cripple me, remember?" He lifts an eyebrow and sneers, daring me to contradict him.

"Don't waste time with him." Nicole pokes me with her finger. "What happened between you and Barney?"

"Get off the warpath, Nikki. You don't own me. It's not your business."

"It is if you diss me with some nobody. The Barn-girl is running around boasting she spent Monday night with you."

"Not the whole night." Barney's shaky voice rises above the crowd.

My mouth goes dry. I look over Nicole's shoulder. Barney approaches, moving slowly, favoring her left leg. She looks the way I once felt after one of Kasili's killer practices. Serves her right for blabbing when I told her to keep it zipped.

"Not the whole night," she repeats in a breathless voice. She stops a few feet behind Nicole.

"No one's talking to you, Barn-girl," Nicole yells.

Barney's gaze falls to the floor.

"Best night of my life." I step around Nicole and move close enough to take Barney's arm. "This girl really knows how to show a guy a good time."

Nicole gasps. "You mean you really did it? You cheated on me with that miserable excuse for a girl?"

Barney stiffens and her hands curl into fists. I consider stepping aside and watching the two girls go after each other. I mean, what guy doesn't love a good cat fight? Instead, I tighten my grip on Barney's arm to keep her close.

Someone snickers. A foot swipes the floor. Nicole looks at me for a second. She seems to be thinking about saying something more. Then she makes up her mind and half-runs down the hall.

The warning bell rings. Spencer lurches away, still surrounded by his group of girls. As he hobbles by, I notice a cloth peeking from his back pocket. A subtle touch. Gang colors aren't permitted inside school. Looks like Spencer decided to join and found a way to declare his allegiance in front of everyone, including our death-to-gangs vice principal. Other students look reluctant to go, but head for their classrooms.

Barney starts to leave.

"Stay," I say.

"Is that an order?" Barney asks.

"Of course…not."

"Hurt you to say that 'not,' didn't it?"

She has no idea.

A shaky freshman stops in front of us. In the squeaky voice of a kid who hasn't hit puberty yet, he says, "Nice going, hero." He's the kind of guy I'd never give permission to talk to me or even look at me.

I shrug. "Anybody can face down Henderson."

"No, I mean, its about what you did for Barney. Nice going." He holds up a hand for a high five.

For a second, the look in his eyes—admiration—makes me square my chest. Then I remember I don't want anyone admiring me. Fear, yes. Respect, even better. Hero-worship—never.

"Run off or I snatch your eyes and shove them down your pathetic throat." I slam my fist into a locker. My knuckles ache, but the noise makes him duck his head and scurry down the hall.

"Why did you do that?" Barney asks.

"That was your fault. You were supposed to keep quiet."

"I know things would have ended differently without you. I think people should know you could be a hero. People hate you around here; don't you care?"

"Maybe I want people hating me."

"Bull." She shakes her head. "No one likes being hated."

"Respected, then. I have a reputation in this place."

"I know you're a certified bad-boy, but is that really enough for you? Why forbid me telling people what you did and almost bite me when I call you hero?"

"Aw, giant, you'd enjoy my bite." I lean over her and gnash my teeth.

"Stop trying to make me angry so you can change the subject." She scowls like a coach squaring off with the refs over a crappy call, and I wonder how she knew what I was trying to do. "I didn't sleep much after what happened. Maybe that's how I lost control, and maybe I exaggerated a little."

"Exaggerated how?"

"Nicole cornered me in the bathroom about my bruises." Barney speaks softly, but at least looks me in the face instead of doing her usual job of staring at the floor. "When I said I had a hard time, she thought I meant with a guy." She swallows and then adds, "She laughed and called me a liar and said no guy would waste a hard time on someone like me and I get so tired of that Barn-girl thing and I went a little crazy and I sort of made her think you and I were out on a date and you fought for me and then we made out." She says it all without breathing.

It wasn't a waste. I bite my tongue to hold back that confession.

*

When the last bell rings to end the day that's dragged on into forever, I remain in my seat. I can't believe I was happy to come back to this place. I still need to clear out my things from the varsity locker room. I could wait until the guys are out on the court practicing. But that would feel like I was running and hiding. I gather my things and head for the gym. I'll do it now. Go in there and be one of the guys one last time.

Silence descends like a hammer when I walk through the locker room doors. I halt at the end of the aisle, fighting down the urge to back out. My teammates—former teammates—look as tense as when we wait at the line for an opposing player to take a final second free throw. That's me. The opposing player.

"Malik." Cesare steps toward me. When I shake my head, he frowns, but he obeys my unspoken command and stays back.

I walk down the aisle, banging my fist on locker doors as I pass. The clangs fill the ugly silence. The guys step aside, giving me plenty of room until I reach the locker labeled with a piece of tape that says Kaplan. I tear at the end of the tape. It's stuck so tight it rips, making a sound that fills the room. I'm left with only half my name in my hands.

I hear heavy breathing behind me. I look and see acting captain Julian Morales invading my space. His hands hang by his side. Now he gets to drop the "acting" part of the title and take control. Like my granddad says, once you're down, people jump to snatch what's yours. The rest of the guys all pretend they're not watching us.

"Back off." My muscles tighten. "I'm not looking for a date."

"What makes you keep doing things you don't want to?"

"I never do anything unless I want to."

"You saying you wanted off the team?" Julian folds his arms over his chest. His lips form a tight line. I know he's laughing at me on the inside, where it counts.

"You get to be number one; just what you wanted. Or is that your problem, being point man when things head downhill without me?"

"Maybe we'll lose some without you, but that happened with you too." Julian squares his shoulders and returns to his locker to finish changing for practice.

The other guys unfreeze and go back to talking. The words swirl around me, but do not include me. Even Cesare rubs his forehead and looks away.

I turn my back on all of them, unzip my gym bag, and begin stuffing my possessions inside. I give Julian a shoulder-shiver as I pass him. Our eyes meet. I take a deep breath, waiting for his counterattack. Instead, he gives a tired shrug and moves aside, out of my path.

As I step out of the locker room door, I hear the ripping noise again. I look back to see Julian completing the job of removing my name.

CHAPTER 16

Fourth period is my free time. Technically, it's a study hall, but no upper classman ever goes to those rooms. I head for the weight room. I work until my muscles burn and sweat pours from my body. The wound in my side barely stings as I punish my muscles, urging them to the edge of breakdown. No one dares to bother me.

When I finish lifting, I go to the gym for a couple of cool-down laps. I circle the inside track and watch teachers send students through their paces.

Today is haul-your-bod-up-the-rope day for the sophomore gym classes. The skinny guys easily move up and down the knotted ropes hanging from the ceiling. The heavy-set kid who's been trying to work his way up one of the ropes for the past three minutes probably wishes he had remained in bed today. Bet he feels trapped by the board of education P.E. requirement. No way he doesn't know how ridiculous he looks, hanging up there with his T-shirt riding up his back, and too-tight shorts clinging to thighs that quiver like chocolate gelatin. Other students around the gym taunt him. The gym teachers are supposed to keep things under control, but the guy in charge of this class must need a hearing aid. As the kid inches his way to the halfway point, the smack talk from the other guys grows louder.

"Shouldn't the fat fag be in class with the girls?"

"How does he live with himself?"

"Put him in a body-bag, if they can find one big enough."

"Hope they're one-size-fits-all."

"This century, fat boy."

Fat boy.

The boy I used to be.

The boy on the rope, the fat boy I used to be, pretends he doesn't hear. Pretends the words don't fester and burn. Sticks and stones break bones. Knives rip through skin and muscle. Words flay you alive and drop you in a vat of acid.

"Move it, slappy-thighs," one guy yells. His nasty chuckle reminds me of the sounds made by the guys who once backed me into dark corners when I was in grade school.

I should be part of this. I'm the badass; I'm supposed to be leading these guys. I should point at the kid on the rope and yell something.

"That's enough," I say.

He whirls to face me. His eyes are wide, as if he's afraid some teacher has decided to step in. Then he recognizes me. His coffee-colored face relaxes and he grins. "Malik, man, I heard you were back. What's up?"

You, if you don't stop.

Henderson is right. I am dangerous.

"Just zip it," I say.

"Come on, Malik, some guys just demand you pick on them." He nudges me and grins, obviously expecting me to tell him he's right. His elbow hits my wound.

"I said shut the hell up!"

His grin disappears. He shuffles away in silence. Other guys stare or follow him. The teacher finally develops hearing and points a finger at me. "We don't tolerate that kind of language in school."

The guy inching up the rope is past the halfway point. Maybe he does look ridiculous. He also looks brave. He's more courageous, more real than me.

"Make it," I mutter. "Do it."

This kid is humiliated every day, but he keeps coming back. It doesn't matter what he looks like on the outside. He's not what the other guys think he is. He's not weak. He won't be stopped.

Until he loses his grip, slides down the rope and hits the floor with a loud thump.

I didn't realize I was holding my breath until the ache in my chest forces me to inhale.

CHAPTER 17

What did my dad say?" I ask the lawyer. Mr. Peterson and my father went before the judge to talk about my "progress." Lack of progress, anyway. It's nearly Christmas and still no essay.

"Almost nothing."

Figures.

"Your father had the sense to let his attorney do the taking." Peterson gives me the same stare he gave the judge in court, like he's trying to pick my brain. "You need to have enough sense to do the writing. It's only five hundred words. I got you an extension this time, but that won't happen again."

"I'm back in school now, you know. Lots of papers to write."

"No bullshit. You know what the judge wants to see. Get it done."

"Yeah, yeah, I'll do it." *Sometime in my next life. Or the one after.*

Strange to think my father once wanted to be in a place like this. Dad has a way bigger office. This place is all books and papers. Two desks are crammed into a space smaller than my bedroom. He's the only one here now. No secretary or executive assistant—Dad beat him there too. Of course, Dad has to show off. Peterson gets to strut in court. I came here to find out what's going on. No point asking Dad anything; I don't need a lecture.

"What's so special about being a lawyer?" I ask. "I mean, look at you; there's nothing special about you."

"Thank you for sharing, Malik." He leans back in his chair with a twisted smile.

"Don't pretend to be mad; you know what I mean." Sometimes you just have to say the truth.

He smiles. "Actually, I do know, and even I agree there's nothing special about me, other than my handsome face and charming wit. Being a lawyer means I have all kinds of arcane knowledge and not much else."

"Arcane?"

"Means I know all the heavy-duty words and how to bullshit a judge," he explains. "I like the job. It's like being in a war without the weapons of mass destruction. You know, like in the old days, when a king would send his champion out to defeat the other guy's best man. Or woman; I have to remember the best might be a she. That's me, my clients' champion." His loud laughter drowns out the sound of the coffee machine.

"Your clients are kings?"

"Don't you consider yourself important?"

I consider myself in need of my car. I wonder if he would sue my dad for me? If he can handle a judge, he can handle my jellyfish father.

I have to get my car back.

*

I see her parked in front of Kaplan's Auto Shop #1 with a big red FOR SALE sign in the windshield. I step inside the shop.

The smell of oil and gasoline is so familiar that I am swamped with a hundred memories. Perry and I used to come here almost every day when I was little. I hung underfoot, trying to be part of everything. Dad and I played a game. He would call for a tool. No matter what he said, I always handed him a wrench and he acted like it was exactly what he wanted. I never got tired of the game and he never sent me away; Perry was the only one who sneered.

When Dad first bought the place from his boss, he kept working side-by-side with the other mechanics. Money was tight; Mom kept the books, answered calls, and stayed in the back where customers couldn't see her. By the time I was old enough to really be useful, things were different. Dad owned several shops and had begun flipping houses: buy cheap, slap on a little paint, and sell high. We moved into the new house and I was kept away from the repair bay. Perry was the Kaplan of the future. Things were all about him, keeping him in line, dealing with his problems. My father, the man who once rolled up his sleeves and worked on hot engines, became a stranger to me. Now he sits upstairs in his office and ignores his minions, the men and women he used to work shoulder-to-shoulder with.

I head up the stairs to the office—corporate headquarters—while trying to make a deal with God.

Get me my car back and I'll go to Mass every Sunday and Temple every Sabbath for at least a month. Maybe two months. Seriously.

"You handle the schedule," I tell Wanda Masters, Dad's executive assistant. I'm willing to work. I'm good, better than some of the employees. I know the physics of engines, the principles of aerodynamics, and the requirements for speed. "Help me out. I need to work and make enough to get my car back before some big shot opens his wallet and drives her away."

"I'm really sorry," she says.

"He has six shops. There has to be something for me somewhere."

"There's nothing, unless you want to take over my position here when I start maternity leave." She leans back in her chair and pats her bulging stomach. She's eight months pregnant with twins and barely fits behind her desk.

I'm almost desperate enough to agree.

"Let me talk to Dad," I say instead.

"He's in a meeting right now."

"I'll wait." He's always in a meeting, unless he's out of town, or just busy and can't be disturbed.

My cellphone buzzes. I don't bother looking. I know it's just another "WRU?" text from Nicole.

Wanda climbs to her feet, using both hands to get out of her chair. Her stomach leads the way across the office to a box sitting on a shelf.

"Do women always get so big when they're pregnant?" I ask.

"Just because I'm growing an entire platoon in here doesn't mean you can't have a little tact." She pats her too-full stomach.

"I know how to tell a lady she's fine." I wonder why things can't be this easy when I'm with the girls at school. There, life is all about image. I can't let people, especially girls, get too close or know too much about me. With Wanda, I can tell a joke and not worry that tomorrow everyone will say Malik acted like an idiot.

"I feel the sincerity, Mr. Player." She clucks like an old woman. "Just answer me one question. If you tell every girl she's fine, what happens when you meet one who really is? How do you get her to trust you?"

"Why do *I* need a girl's trust?"

Instead of answering, her eyes widen. She touches her stomach and murmurs, "Oh, my."

"Are they coming?" My mouth becomes a desert. "Should I call Simon?" Her husband works downstairs.

"Relax," Wanda says. "I just got kicked. I think one or both woke up and decided to go for a jog. Would you like to feel?"

"No! No way."

But she holds her hand out to me and lifts an eyebrow in invitation. I step closer. I let her take my hand and pull it to her stomach. At first all I feel is the material of her shirt. Then something presses against my palm. I step back and rub my hand against my jeans.

"They're really in there," I say.

"Everything changes when one plus one makes three." She smiles, a look that seems happy and sad at the same time. "Well, for my husband and me, it makes four. I told him he was finally going to have to grow up. I intended to come back to work right away, but now I don't know. I didn't count on twins."

The door of the office opens. Good old Dad steps out. He looks like a guy hawking some amazing deal on a late-night infomercial. Makes me wonder why he bothers hiring actors for the Kaplan Auto Parts and Body Shop commercials. At least he never made his family stand in front of the cameras. Perry would have loved that. I would have shriveled up and died.

Another man follows Dad. He wears a dark blue suit and a yellow power tie, and looks like some big-time music label's A&R manager scouting out new talent. He is taller than Dad, and older. But somehow my father seems to dwarf him.

The man points at me. "Is this your boy, Dwayne?"

Dad's tight nod and averted glance reveals his reluctance to claim me—even now, when I'm all he has left.

Look at me, Dad. Look at me.

Look. At. Me.

He doesn't. I shouldn't care anymore. I hate that I do.

"I'm Walter Lotspeich from Alderman Whyte's office," Dad's companion says, as he shakes my hand. "The alderman and I both follow the Farrington team you're leading to glory."

"You can't be following too close," I say. Lotspeich? Tell me he's kidding. He can't actually live with that name.

"Excuse me?" Lotspeich blinks.

"Malik had an…incident. He's no longer on the team." Dad glances at me for a second as he speaks. His lips tighten like he's bitten into something rotten and is struggling to keep from spitting it back out.

I finally got Dad to notice me.

Only he hated what he saw.

Lotspeich slaps my shoulder. "Well, life happens, right? Do me a favor and talk this man into saying yes to our proposition. Alderman Whyte needs him."

"The alderman needs the auto guy?" I use the sarcastic nickname Mom's family gave Dad years ago. "Does he want his limo detailed?"

Anger flares behind Dad's plastic smile. Every muscle looks like stone, and his breathing becomes loud and fast, whistling through his nose. He says nothing, just stares. I brace for the explosion. Maybe this time Dad won't be the soft jellyfish.

"Limo detailed? Good one." Lotspeich laughs and turns to Dad. "You never said your son was such a jokester."

He leaves. I realize too late that he takes my chance with him. Dad couldn't have refused me, not with the alderman's representative standing there and listening. Instead of being smart, I let my tongue say what it wanted. There's no point going in the office to talk to my dad now.

Dad turns his head away, as if he can't stand looking at me another moment. He returns to his office, closing the door softly behind him. He can't even stand being in the same room.

Wanda throws me a dirty look.

If I had a mirror, I'd do the same.

CHAPTER 18

Cesare and I are at his apartment, exchanging presents. He lives above a bakery. The smell of freshly baked bread flows through the window. When I rip off the brown paper covering the package he hands me, I find a book: <u>An Idiot's Guide to Being God</u>. There is also a note: *Check out page sixty-nine.*

At first I think it's a joke. I'm ready for pretty much anything except the two sentences he underlined.

We are neither superhuman nor magical. Feeling powerless is an occasional and unfortunate fact of life. We prove ourselves by what we do afterwards.

Who else knows me so well?

"I'm giving you the best present ever," I say. "Tomorrow night, you and me are heading out to Ageless Encounters." Ageless is a night club that recently opened up only a few miles from my house. The name really means twenty-one and up.

"That's a club. You can't get in that place," he says.

"Don't forget who you're talking to." I pull two special passes from my back pocket. "I can do anything."

"How'd you score those?" He stares at the passes, but doesn't move when I extend one to him. "This is your uncle's doing, isn't it?"

"What, I can't set things up myself?" Then I admit, "He finally got a new job; he's their new 'security specialist.'" Leon Kaplan, my dad's older brother, is an army vet. He's a fun guy who believes in living large.

"You mean he's a bouncer?"

Who cares what you call it, he has a job? "All we have to do is dress to impress and he'll wave us through the door."

"Why not take Nicole?"

"You don't take a girl to a club, man; that's just wrong. We're going to meet new girls, you know, that babe-shopping thing. Don't wimp out on me, man."

Cesare draws in a deep breath. "I can't go."

"You have to."

"I can't."

"Just tell your girl something came up; she can miss you for one night."

"It not Giselle; it's my parents."

Why is Cesare making this so hard? The routine is simple. He comes to my place to spend the night. I snarl at my parents, say we want to be alone, and slam my bedroom door. They don't bother us again. We sneak out the basement window, where I jimmied the alarm, and hustle over to Ageless. We enjoy the night, sneak back inside before dawn, and it's all good.

Cesare bites his lower lip and considers. Then he shakes his head. "I don't want to lie to my dad. I promised I'd stay out of trouble."

"He won't ever know, ditwad. He's on the road. When's he due back?"

"Not until New Year's."

"So he's no problem."

Cesare's not fun the way he's always been before. His lips go tight, his shoulders square, and he shakes his head. "I can't do it, Malik. I gave him my word. He keeps saying I need to be more responsible." Cesare looks like he's aged years in the past week.

"Bet he says a lot more, like stop hanging with that Kaplan boy." A bitter taste fills my mouth.

"No." Then Cesare nods and admits, "Well, yes, but I never listen to that stuff. You and me, we're a team—Russo and Kaplan."

"Kaplan and Russo, man, and we're supposed to watch out for each other. You can't let your old man come between us." I won't have fun alone, can't he see that? "I need my wing man. You have to come and keep me from getting too wasted. Think about it: music, lights, drinks. And girls. Older girls." I hit him on the chest and leer. "College girls."

"I don't need a college girl. I'm not going. Dad gave up gambling for us. I'm going to do this for him." He crosses his arms and lifts his chin with unmistakable attitude.

"Fine." I brush my hands on my pants. "Then I'll go alone."

"What about your curfew?"

That's a dumbass question. "I won't stay at home like a scared little boy, just so my old man won't bust me for breaking a curfew I only have because you thought Spencer insulted you."

"Giselle. He insulted my girl." Cesare shakes his head. His eyes look like two shards of ice. "My dad doesn't want me around you. He'd throw a fit if you spent the night here. You can't stay here and I can't go with you."

"Your father's on the road; he's gone more than he's around. He's given us flack before. So has mine, and we've always ignored them."

"He's serious this time. And Mom, I hear her pacing and talking to herself when she doesn't know I'm around. I can't jeopardize my chances, not now." Cesare won't meet my eye, and his voice sounds flat, like he's reciting a speech. "It's stupid to take chances."

Stupid! I'm the only reason he's still on the court, the reason the Illinois coach still wants him. The University of Illinois rescinded their offer to me the day the judge rendered his verdict. Others colleges quickly followed suit. But I won't let that stop me. I will be a Fighting Illini. And I will have a good time tonight, no matter what.

"Stupid is me having to run along home every night. You can't toss nine years aside because daddy told you to."

"My parents expect things from me. My sisters and brother expect things. And Giselle—I love the girl. Her mother will make her dump me if I keep getting in trouble."

"Your folks, your girl. Better get yourself a dog so you can blame him next." I step back and flip him off.

Cesare reaches for me.

"Keep your distance. You don't want to piss off your old man."

Screw Cesare and my damned curfew. I grab my jacket and race down the stairs and back to the cold outside. I'm going out to find people who want what I have to give.

Granddad was right. Friendship is just a disguise.

I need Ageless more than ever.

CHAPTER 19

Loud music pulses through the air outside the closed doors of the club. I'm dressed in a red-and-black skulled Ed Hardy shirt and black jeans, and my dark glasses. A long line of noisy bodies waits in the cold for Security Specialist Leon Kaplan to let them inside. He looks about as fierce as a beardless black Santa in a tight red jacket that outlines his bulging stomach. Uncle Leon had to repeat eighth grade. That meant he and Dad went through high school together. He rushed off to join the army after graduation, missing my parents' wedding. His years in the military left him with a strut in his walk and an attitude that makes him perfect for this job. Night work is good because he hates mornings. He gets to flirt with girls and have all the free drinks he can handle. All he has to do is look ferocious. He's a natural; maybe he finally has a job he can keep longer than a few months.

Right now he's talking with a pair of giggling girls trying to wiggle their way past the line waiting for admittance. A tall white girl with blond hair and her dark-skinned friend. From behind my reflective Ray-Bans, I watch these girls use every exposed weapon they possess. The girls' short coats hang open. Both are dressed to impress and display sky-high heels and tight clothes. The green strapless dress on the blonde must be held up by glue. The black girl wears a plunging honey-colored blouse over dark brown flared pants. The breeze carries their perfumes, something flowery and sweet. If I stood guard at the door I'd have let them have whatever they wanted long ago.

Uncle Leon's puffy lips tighten into a stern line when he sees me.

"Excuse me, ladies; we have a VIP among us."

"OMG, are you him?" the black girl says. I wonder who she thinks I am. She moves closer to me and links her arm with mine. I decide I don't really care; not as long as she keeps rubbing her fine self against me.

"I'm incognito," I tell her. I look pointedly at a sign in the window, which says Horst and Enemies of Blood and Flesh will be playing at Ageless in a few weeks.

"I'll keep your secret, Horst." She places her head on my shoulder.

Her vanilla friend seems skeptical. "Horst never goes out without bodyguards." The blonde crosses her arms over her chest, pushing her breasts up. That industrial strength glue continues holding.

Putting a finger to my lips, I say, "Now ladies, I don't want a big fuss. Haven't you ever wanted to just get out on your own, dump the entourage, slip free, and meet real people?"

Uncle Leon gives me a look. I wonder if he realizes I'm not lying. Sometimes I really do wish I could just relax, be smooth, and forget about living up to my reputation. At least tonight I can dance, drink, and forget.

My uncle laughs. "That Horst, he's something else, eh, ladies? He's scouting the place out before his group comes to perform."

I look at the girls, place a hand over my heart, and bow. "Ladies, would you like to be my guests?" Who says I have no tact?

They look at each other and giggle. Then each grabs one of my arms. Leon waves me and the girls through the door. Once inside, the girls release me. They link arms with each other and begin walking into the crowd.

"Wait a minute," I say. I have to yell to hear myself over the noise. "Ladies, you can't just leave Horst."

Vanilla stops and looks back. "I wouldn't. But you're not him. We're inside; that's all that matters."

The other girl nods. "I mean, thanks, whoever you are, but we got plans for tonight that don't include a nobody. Oh, and you need to lose the dark glasses. They make you look ridiculous." The girls melt into the noisy crowd.

I stop in the men's room, pull off my glasses, and stare into the mirror. I'm not Horst the rapper. I don't look like him. I barely look like myself. In the strained light of the single bulb hanging from the ceiling, my face is distorted. Usually, I feel exposed without my glasses, but the girl was right. I was a fool to wear them tonight. The glasses go in my pocket; this place is my disguise.

"Let the fun begin," I mutter, and head for the dance floor. Give me a few drinks and I won't care about either of those girls.

Pretty soon, I get next to a tall girl who calls herself Angelica. Her dark hair is piled on her head, exposing her neck and shoulders and a tight top that bulges and shakes like it's filled with Jell-O. She agrees to a dance that sets the Jell-O jiggling. Angelica almost makes me ache for college.

Until she spends the dance complaining about some guy who just dumped her. I don't blame him. A body only makes up for so much, and her mouth won't stop. I applaud the guy for putting up with her for three weeks, two days, and seven hours.

"And seven hours, can you believe that? And then he just up and says goodbye. I keep finding the wrong guys; men who don't believe in commitment. He gave me the whole, 'It's not you, it's me' speech. Better believe it wasn't me. It was awful to get dumped when I put every-thing into that relationship." She pauses and I search for an escape route. Then she sobs and adds, "Why couldn't he want my brain?"

I'm not touching that one. Her brain, I mean. I nod and feign sympathy before sidling away and heading to one of the bars. The bar-tender frowns until I flash the fake ID that makes me twenty-two. I order a drink. "Beer. Whatever you have on tap."

The bartender returns with a mug filled with golden brew, topped by an inviting frothy head that is a tribute to the bartender's skill and the quality of the place. I lift the cold mug, breathe in the scent, and feel the bubbles on my lips.

The bartender looks over my shoulder and waves, saying, "The usual, Zach?"

"You know it, Roberto," a familiar voice says. "Nice seeing you again, Malik."

Oh hell!

I put my beer back on the counter and try pretending I have no idea who it belongs to. I turn to see a face I had hoped I'd never need to see again: Mr. Patterson, Dad's lawyer. His tailored suit has been replaced by rumpled pants, a muscle shirt that reveals a huge tattoo of an eagle on his right shoulder, and a load of chains around his neck. The outfit screams "I'm here to party." I didn't know lawyers were allowed to dress like that.

"Should you be here?" Zach asks. I can't think of him as Mr. Patterson in those clothes.

"Should you?" Defiance tightens my voice. I can't help staring at the tattoo. It's not an Enforcer tombstone, but why would a stuffed suit have any ink? Or be in a place like this?

Tonight of all nights.

I am so busted.

CHAPTER 20

W hy aren't you busting me?"

Zach is a lawyer; can he sit by and watch a crime being committed, even if I am a client? Then I think, he is *my* lawyer. That means he can't turn me in, no matter what I do. I relax and say, "What I do is confidential, right? That's the way it works when you have a client, right?"

Zach groans. "Unlike your old man, who knows his stuff, what you don't know about the law and lawyers would fill this room. But then, you thought being seventeen would keep you out of trouble, didn't you?" In spite of his words, something in his expression tells me I matter to Zach.

The bartender returns and places a glass on the counter in front of Zach. The liquid inside is clear, with tiny bubbles on the sides. "Here you are, seltzer water with lime."

"You come to a place like this to drink water?" I ask when the bartender leaves.

"With lime." Zach lifts the glass and an eyebrow. "I used to drink like a fish, and none of it water. Of course, I was a card-carrying alcoholic back then. Martinis, whiskey, rum, beer, you name it, I drowned in it. These days, I'm more selective."

"I've seen alkies; you don't look like one." What kind of a man disses himself like that out loud in a place where anyone could overhear? I've seen drunks and winos on the streets. Sloppy drunks with glazed eyes who smell like toilets and talk to themselves without the excuse of a bluetooth. There were a few in the jail, looking miserable. I even see guys who are already half-past wasted in here. Zach isn't acting like one of them.

His lips twitch like he's fighting to hold back laughter. "Bloodshot eyes, shaking hands, unshaven…that's just the stereotype. By the way, the word is alcoholic, not alkie, and we're all over. We look like everyone. Even lawyers and high school students."

He picks up his glass and starts walking away. This is my chance to disappear into the crowd. Instead, I try imagining my father here with me. No chance he'd ever talk to me like this, like I'm an adult, like I'm important. I grab my beer and follow the eagle.

"Are you sure you're a real lawyer?" I ask.

"I got your ass off without jail time, didn't I? Feel free to applaud my efforts." He looks over his shoulder and shows his teeth in a wicked grin. "These clothes, the tattoo, they display my dark side. I didn't kick all my bad habits when I decided to sober up."

He stops at a small table where three men sit and points me to an empty chair. He then grabs a chair from another table and sits next to me. "Malik, let me introduce my pals: Barry Sanders," a guy with a glass of scotch and the shoulders and arms of a professional body-builder gives a wave, "Enrico Chavez," a Hispanic man with a thin moustache lifts a glass filled with an amber liquid I can't identify, "and Bill Smith."

"And that is my for-real name," Bill says as he shakes my hand. Him I understand. He has a beer in front of him.

"Guys, this is Malik Kaplan." As I shake hands with the other two, Zach continues, "Barry's a former client, like you. Bill works in the law office with me, and Chavez, for his sins, is my brother-in-law. He's also into the whole your-body-is-a-temple crap. Be careful or he'll have you going vegan."

"It's not crap." Chavez points a finger at Zach. "I listen to my doc so I'll live to be a hundred, easy."

"A long life maybe, but will it be worthwhile?" Barry asks. "What happens if you go out that door and get hit by a bus?"

"You are what you eat and drink," Chavez insists. "You have to take care of yourself. Me, I drink herbal tea, no coffee, and no caffeine-hyped soft drinks."

"Tea mixed with a little Kahlua," Barry stage whispers like he's revealing a national secret.

Chavez takes a drink from his glass and runs his tongue over his thin lips. "A few drops only. A man's allowed a little indulgence."

"Why are they drinking?" I whisper to Zach.

"My friends aren't alcoholics." Zach doesn't lower his voice. He points at his own skull and says, "I am. That's why I like this place; Roberto knows how to make all the best mocktails: the Designated Appletini, the Hot Not Toddy, and even an old fashioned Virgin Miami Vice. Or good old seltzer with lime." He lifts his glass in a half-salute. Then he points at the men around the table. "As for these three, they aren't even problem drinkers. I've seen old Barry down a half a glass of scotch and then leave the rest behind. Go figure."

Barry shakes his head. "Zach acts like that's some kind of miracle. I take what I need and leave the rest."

"See, they could all get up and go home right now. They don't feel a need to keep drinking as long as the liquor supply holds out. Me, I'm different, and I know it. I lost Ronnie, my first wife, because she couldn't handle life with me."

"Then she didn't deserve you," I say.

Zach stares down into his glass and sighs. "She deserved better. I don't blame her for growing tired of me back then. I grew tired of the me I was."

"She wouldn't let you drink at all?"

"You don't get it. That poor girl didn't *let* me drink; she couldn't stop me. No one could. I came from a family of brilliant minds, and they all tried. 'Just drink a couple, drink slowly, only drink beer…'"

I've heard the same things. I remember every lecture. Use your willpower. Just say no. Be strong. It's your choice.

My father's voice: *Have you learned nothing from watching your grandfather?*

"Truth is, a few drops of alcohol and poof." Zach wiggles his fingers in the air like a magician preparing to reach into a magic hat. "I go brain dead and I don't stop until there's nothing left. I ruined any chance of a relationship with a lot of people. Good people. Nothing helped until I crashed and hit bottom."

I don't understand how he can sit here with his friends and his brother-in-law listening and pretend there is something wrong with his brain. In-laws are brutal. Mom's brothers never waste an opportunity to tear into Dad. I should never have called him the auto guy. That's their spiteful name for him.

I saw Zach handle the judge and prosecutor. He was large and in charge, in control of himself and everyone else, like a perfectly tuned motor. He likes alcohol, big flying whoop. Zach also likes pasta a little too much and dresses too old school. Way too old school; he needs a better shirt. But all that means nothing. There is *nothing* wrong with his brain.

"If you can't drink or have fun, why come to a club?" I ask.

"Who says I don't have fun? I'm a recovering alcoholic, not a stoic. Took years before I could handle places like this, but now I can see booze, I can even smell it, and I'm still fine. Truth is, my friends like to come here, and I like to be with my friends. It's kind of like poking a bruise. It hurts, but it's a good hurt, y'know? I get my kicks watching these dudes who have no idea how ridiculous they look after tossing down a few."

"We know." Bill drinks, belches, and licks foam from the back of his hand like a thirsty dog. "We just don't care."

Instead of laughing, Zach sighs and looks at his hands. "Since I began my recovery, I've found a new wife, one who understands that Al-Anon is her best friend. I've made new friends, and these are three of the best. They've got standing orders to knock me upside the head if I touch a drop of the hard stuff, and I know Chavez would land the first blow, with Bill and Barry fighting for second place."

"Damn straight," Chavez says and makes a fist.

"That's what friends are for," Barry adds.

"I like my head, so I choose no booze." Zach takes a drink of his seltzer water. "Life is good now, but I still look back at what I threw away. That reminds me to be super careful with my second chance."

"You need these guys to make you stop? Don't you have willpower?"

Zach stares at me. "Do you? Have willpower, I mean."

"I'm not weak."

"I never said you were. But not long ago, you got so drunk you ended up in jail. Now you're sneaking in here to drink again even after my warning. You worry me. I should be a concerned adult, take that drink from you, and march you out of here. Or contact the police."

"But you won't."

"No." He points through the crowd at the bartender. "I'm not get-ting Roberto in trouble because he's overworked and you're out with what is probably an excellent fake ID. But I fear you are just like me. An alcoholic."

"No way." *Not me. Never.*

"I hope not. Because waiting to hit bottom is a hell of a life. But if you are, I can't stop you. I can only tell you what it's like for me." He pulls a card from his pocket and scribbles on it as he talks. "I belong to Alcoholics Anonymous and my home group is my lifeline. If I even think about drinking I remember I'll have to face them and confess." He takes another sip from his glass and grimaces. "Scares the urge to imbibe right out of me. It was a battle, but I've learned to love seltzer water. The lime makes all the difference."

"That's you, not me. I went to a party, had a couple of beers, and I got angry. I don't have an alcohol problem."

"No one does, until suddenly they do. Until they have no friends left, no one to loan them money or to steal from."

"I don't borrow or steal."

Zach chokes as if he's trying not to laugh out loud. "No, you're unlucky enough to have money. Just means you'll fall from a higher place before you hit bottom. I know. It's what happened to me."

"I'm not you."

"Obviously. Here's the trick." His voice grows even lower, like he's about to tell me the secret of life. I bend close and smell the lime on his breath. "If you can have one beer and walk away with money in your pocket, the glass only half empty, and no regrets, I'd say you're right, you have no problem."

"You're trying some kind of trick on me."

"No trick; at least not one I was ever successful with." Zach lifts his glass and the lime swirls in the liquid.

I pick up my beer mug. The glass remains cold, but the head is gone. What's left inside tastes a little flat, but still goes down smooth as butter. After swallowing half, I return the mug to the table. Several drops spill. I frown at the loss before lifting my hands in the air and leaning back in my chair. "See, I stopped. With beer still in my glass and money in my pocket."

Zach doesn't look impressed. "You're still sitting there. Plenty of time for you to have more."

I remain at the table long after Zach and his friends leave, staring at my glass. The beer is still flat, but the feeling of loss disappears when I finish off the last of the drink.

Almost as soon as Zach and his friends have gone, a tall Latina joins me. She calls herself Rosaria. Her fingers curl around a glass of red wine darker than her fingernail polish.

"Are you sure you're old enough to be in this place?" Her eyes sparkle as she talks, almost like she's laughing at me.

"I've got good genes. The men in my family stay young and healthy forever." I flex my arms.

She laughs. "Well, you do look like you work out."

"Every day, babe. Got to be the best me I can, you know what I'm saying?" My brain shifts into second gear. I find all the right things to say as I race down the speedway toward the turn. I stare deep into her eyes. "I love Chicago State, but life is about more than studies."

She sips her wine and moves closer to me. "Is that where you go to school?"

"Go Cougars," I say, pleased that I remembered Chicago State University's mascot.

"What are you drinking?" Rosaria asks. Her shirt is so yellow I have to blink, even in the club's dim lights. She smells good too, not too sweet and perfumed. I can't act like some kid, not when I'm around a girl like this. I'm not ordering a virgin anything. Not even seltzer water.

I wave at the bartender. "I'll have what she's having."

It's only wine. That barely counts.

CHAPTER 21

I've got Rosaria's number plugged into my phone, along with a few others, by the time Uncle Leon's shift ends and he drives me home. It's almost dawn on Sunday when I climb back through the basement window. The guy who installed the expensive, high-tech security system called it foolproof. Not being a fool, I easily disable the equipment and get in and out through the basement window anytime I want. I feel shaky and tired, a little buzzed, and lucky I know the basement so well I don't have to think too hard to find my way in the dark.

The familiar smell of Dad's cigar tells me I'm not alone a moment before the lights snap on. I blink in the sudden glare. He sits on the ratty old sofa he refused to toss when we moved into this house. He calls it a classic. I'm not sure, but I think the thing is older than me.

Dad keeps all the useless things down here.

"Hey Dad. Relax. I just went out for a walk; I couldn't sleep and…"

"Don't."

"You know Mom will kill you for smoking in the house." I point to the smoldering cigar in the ashtray, trying to distract him.

"This has to stop, Malik."

Son. Call me son.

He lowers his head, pulls a handkerchief from his pocket, and wipes his glasses. He can't even feel angry. It's like I'm just another employee or supplier, someone who needs to be reminded that Kaplan Senior is the boss before being dismissed.

"I'm tired," I say, and head for the stairs.

He stands up from the sofa, moving fast, to get between me and the staircase. He sniffs and curls his lips. "Have you been drinking?"

"No."

"Don't lie. You reek of alcohol."

"Then why'd you bother asking?"

"I don't understand you. You resemble my son, but you're not him."

I can never be Perry. He never spoke this quietly when Perry messed up. My brother never had to doubt our father cared about him. Dad was always on his case, always after him to become something, to make him proud and be his partner. I want Dad to be proud of me. I want to be proud of him.

Two more unavailable choices.

I glance at the corner where what's left of the abandoned Kaplan and Son sign leans, rusting against the wall. Dad made that sign when Perry started his senior year so it would be ready for the graduation that never happened. He took a hammer to the sign the day after Perry's funeral. I guess "and Son" was never meant to apply to me.

"You're not much of a father, either," I say through the sour taste filling my throat. I put my foot on the bottom stair.

"Where do you think you're going?" His voice shakes.

"To bed."

"No."

"What's that supposed to mean?"

"That was a complete sentence and needs no explanation. You stay here and tell me what you've been doing."

Angry words pour from my mouth faster than I can think. "I was out hanging with my gang homies. We went drinking and drugging and whoring and—"

The blow is so swift and sudden that only the pain in my jaw tells me I've been slugged. I never expected this. He's never hit me before.

"Now I know what you really think of me," I say bitterly.

I hear his angry grunt again as he marches past me up the staircase, and I know I've been dismissed. I've never felt so far from him before. I was out to make him angry. I succeeded. Somehow, the sad look on his face doesn't make me feel much like a winner.

*

I follow the smell of breakfast downstairs the next day—no, same day; it's still Sunday. The sunlight pouring through the widows feels like acid on my skin. I only had a few hours of sleep. The inside of my mouth feels like a dentist wedged his rubber glove down my throat. I don't have to look in the bathroom mirror; I know my eyes are bloodshot from the haze surrounding the world. I pop a few Advil, but some demented drummer continues beating inside my skull. And my jaw—Dad definitely looked at me this time. His aim was perfect.

Dad sits at the breakfast table reading the newspaper. He looks up when I enter the kitchen and grunts as he folds his paper and lays it on the table. "How are you feeling?"

"Beat up and slapped around," I say, pouring myself a cup of coffee. I drink it black while leaning against the sink, staring at the wall to shut him out.

He rubs a hand over his forehead and his eyelids droop like he never slept. It's almost noon; why is he still here? Waiting to see me so he can gloat? I touch my jaw, turning my head so he will get a good look at the new bruise his fist left on my face.

"I thought I'd drive your mother to Mass. I could take you, too, if you want to go." The newspaper rustles as he speaks.

"Isn't religion the opium of the people? I thought you didn't want me doing drugs." At least history class is good for one thing. His shudder tells me I scored.

Mom hustles into the kitchen wearing another of her dark brown dresses. She buttons her coat as she walks. A scarf is tied around her head, but nothing hides the look in her eyes when she sees me.

"Who hurt you, baby?" The rough skin of her two-fingered hand brushes across my forehead. She hasn't called me baby in years.

"It's nothing."

"Malik Anderson Kaplan, tell me what happened."

God, not all three names.

"Can't a guy get a cup of coffee in peace without being hassled about every little thing?" I pull away. I want to talk. But if I start I might not be able to stop. The heavy-handed drummer in my head pounds harder. I put down my coffee and say, "I'm heading out."

"Where?" Dad asks.

"I don't know."

His chair scrapes the floor as he stands. He and Mom leave the kitchen together. Minutes later, I hear his car pull out of the garage. He usually drives like he walks, slow and deliberate, as if he doesn't understand that speed limits are advisory. Today, he tears away from the house as if he wants to punish the engine.

Or maybe just punish me.

CHAPTER 22

I hike to the local Community Center in search of something I can punish. The place is packed. Even the skateboard park on the outside is crowded with future X Games competitors who don't care about the cold. The Center almost had to close a few years ago. There's a plaque near the door thanking Anonymous for coughing up funds. It's hard to believe anyone cared enough about this part of the city to play Santa Claus. I remember Perry joking that the check would probably bounce. But it didn't, and apparently Anonymous keeps sending in money, because the doors remain open.

I head for the far end of the building, past the concession area, indoor basketball court, meeting rooms, and rooms for crafts and classes. Only the serious enter the room christened the Anti-Aggression Outlet, a name painted in big red letters on the door.

I begin sweating the moment I walk through the door. The air is stale but familiar, filled with sweat and the body odor that belongs in a room dedicated to boxing. Grunts and pounding fists. Weights and jump ropes. A ring for sparring, a few speed balls on the walls, and two heavy bags. This place, this equipment, and the men inside, changed me from the fat kid into the hard body. This place and Ed, a guy who was old when I first walked through the door. He gave this place its nickname and he repaints the sign on the door every spring. He loves his art too, and wears low-necked t-shirts that display a set of tattoos so vast, an Enforcer's tombstone would get lost in the mix.

"We don't do babysitting," Ed told me my first day. When he bent over me, he flexed his muscles and made the snarling tiger tattoo on his left bicep appear ready to leap across the space between us and devour me. When I didn't run away, everyone started laughing. They never knew I was frozen in fear. I had bitten my tongue, my mouth was filled with blood, and I didn't dare open it. Ed decided I had guts and chose to train me himself.

Now, I wave off an invitation from a guy looking for a sparring partner and attack the heavy bag some joker painted a face on years ago. Sometimes my fist pounds Spencer and sometimes Dreadlocks. Suddenly, my father's face jumps into my mind. I close my eyes and back away from the bag. My arms are shaking, my breathing ragged. I grab a towel to wipe sweat from my head.

I hear voices from across the room.

"They teach that dance-kickboxing stuff down the hall; that's what you want, honey."

I almost laugh at the sound of Ed's growl.

A girl answers him. "I'm not looking for dancing and I'm not your honey."

No, she's Barney.

I pull off my boxing gloves and join the group lounging by the door to watch her argue with Ed.

"This isn't some fitness class where you dance around and throw punches in the air," he says and points at the door. "If you want to watch guys pound on each other, try the school halls." The guys hang back, all waiting to see what she will do next. When the tattooed hulk hands out his "get lost" speech, most girls turn and leave and never come back. Most guys do, too.

Barney puts her hands on her waist. She didn't cry or run in the alley, and she doesn't now. "I have a right to use this gym."

Her black jeans are tight enough to outline her curvy thighs and restrict her movements. Her heavy sweatshirt will have her rolling in sweat in minutes. At least she remembered to wear gym shoes. I can guess why she came, what she's looking for, but she'll never win a fight with a guy like the Enforcer. He manhandled her so easily, I'm surprised she wants to try. I want to put my arm around her. Want to tell her nothing will hurt her again. But I'm one of the people she has to fear.

"Has that guy been back?" I ask.

"No. But I don't want to wait around until he shows up and it's too late. I don't care what you say, I'm going to learn to fight."

"How can I help?"

Her eyes widen. She didn't expect that. I don't believe what I said myself. But I won't take it back.

"I'm here to learn how to really fight," she says.

"If you had tried fighting that guy, you'd have a lot worse than a few bruises." I point at the remains of the angry purple bruise on her neck. "Why not just hire a bodyguard?"

"Are you available?" She gives me an arch look. On any other girl, I would say that look meant she was trying to flirt.

"Then who'll protect you from me?" I take her wrists. She jerks free so fast I almost end up punching myself in the face. I reach for her again. This time my hands tighten so she can't pull away. I feel the thin ridges of the scars on each wrist. She glances at me.

"You guys gonna dance or what?" Ed calls from across the room.

"Or what," I yell back. He snorts. I release Barney's hands and tell her what the physical therapist once told my mother. "You start by being quiet. You listen and do everything I tell you, exactly the way I tell you, no more, no less. I can promise you'll hate me before this is over."

"You mean you'll do it? You'll teach me?" Her head lifts and her smile shows bright, even teeth and deep dimples.

"Didn't I just tell you to listen? How much weight can you press?" Her smile disappears and she remains silent, until I add, "Answer the question."

"I don't know."

I roll my eyes. "Of course you don't. God, girls. Okay, let's go."

We begin with a run around the block to warm up her muscles. I jog with her, keeping the pace slow when I see her favoring one leg. Her shoulder looks iffy, too. But she has endurance and doesn't complain.

"Not bad," I say as we complete the first circuit and start around the block a second time.

"Maybe I can't press, whatever that is, but I'm not a complete fatass." Anger spills from her voice.

"That's not what I meant."

"Most people do." She shrugs and looks down at the ground. She acts the way Mom did after the fire convinced her she was ugly.

"Head up when you run. And look at a guy when you talk to him."

She lets out a noisy breath, but lifts her head. "I'm still trying to work on that. Comes with feeling out of place. Life is easier if you're slim, beautiful, and short."

"I'm taller than you."

"And you're a guy, so it's all good. I'm the biggest girl in school, except for some members of the girls' basketball team."

"Why don't you join?"

"The coach actually stalks me, but I'm an awful player. My brother tried teaching me, but even he had to give up." She lifts her hands. "See, both lefties. I never really wanted to play. I just went to games because I liked watching my brother."

"And Julian." I'm careful to keep my face blank and my voice smooth. I see the two of them together all the time. Barney and Julian are in the same English class, and they eat lunch together. They walk together in the halls, and her dimples show when she smiles at him.

"Julian, too. He's my friend."

I close my mouth to keep from asking what she considers me.

We finish our second circuit. When we reach the entrance again, I take her back inside to the door of the Outlet.

"Are you sure you're serious enough to keep with this for the long haul?" I ask before I open the door.

"Absolutely."

"Don't answer so fast. You have to keep running like this to train your heart. You'll need weight training, and not just once in a while, or only when you feel like it. You'll pump iron, run a thousand laps, do pushups, sit-ups, crunches. You'll punch a bag that feels like a brick wall until your knuckles bleed or your shoulders give out, or both. You'll take hits and be knocked down and end up hurting worse than you do now. And when you've done all that, you still won't be able to take that guy down, or anyone like him."

"Why not? When I get training—"

"You'll know enough to get him mad enough to really kick your ass."

"Are you such a rotten teacher?"

"Any of the guys in there will tell you the same thing. Why do you think so few girls ever step inside that door?"

"Because of the smell?"

I don't do the near-naked chest look Ed loves, but I flex my arms to give Barney a good view of my muscles. "Testosterone. We guys get the muscles you never will." I grab her wrists again. She tries to pull away from me and fails, again. I have to make her understand that she needs to keep clear of the Enforcers. "In the end, a big guy will destroy you, because we're stronger and we like to win. Boxing lessons won't change that."

Her breathing grows faster. Her chest pumps in a way that makes me remember girls do have a secret weapon of their own. A kiss, a touch, hell, even a smile, and estrogen wins.

"Barney..." I release her and step back.

"I have to do something." Her face is all grim determination. "I don't intend on being manhandled again. I'm tired of being pushed around by guys. You, my brother—"

"Saint David bosses you around?"

"Everyone bosses me, but I'm going to do this." She tosses her head and marches inside the Outlet. I surrender and follow her.

CHAPTER 23

Barney starts with conditioning, working her upper body with pushups and crunches. She doesn't complain, but she's going to need a lot of work before she should even think about sparring. That could be a good thing. I have a vision of her trying to fight alone like some vigilante and getting ripped to pieces. The bodyguard thing might be a better idea, except working with her is actually fun.

A few of the guys hassle me as Barney and I prepare to leave. I know jealousy when I see it and remind them, "You had the chance to get to her first."

We approach the concession stand. My stomach grumbles. They have something for every taste here, and the smells fight an international war. Chinese fried rice and egg rolls, Mexican burritos and churros, Jamaican beef patties covered in golden-brown pastry shells and coconut drops, even old-fashioned pizza and fried chicken.

Barney takes a deep breath and licks her lips. "I can't believe I didn't think to bring money."

Workouts obviously strengthen the estrogen effect. I hear myself offering to pay for her. "Get whatever you want, my treat."

She hesitates.

"No strings attached." I cross my heart as I speak.

"Okay, but I'll pay you back tomorrow at school."

She doesn't seem to realize she just insulted me.

In honor of the reggae music pouring from the speakers, I order one of the Jamaican patties, along with a side of red beans and rice. My rumbling stomach demands more, so I add a burrito. Barney orders a pattie. Nothing more.

"Guys get to eat anything," she mutters, as we reach the cashier.

"You can have more," I say, but she shakes her head.

The drinks are kept behind the counter. I turn to the clerk and say, "I want a bottle of ginger beer. Make that two."

Barney frowns as I lead the way to a table. Her jaw clenches hard when I put one of the bottles in front of her. I almost feel knives slicing my skin as she lectures, "I don't drink beer. You shouldn't either."

"You drink root beer, right? This isn't real. They can't sell alcohol in this place."

"Oh. I knew that." A muscle jerks in her jaw as she speaks.

No, she didn't, but it's fun watching her pretend. I take a swig from my bottle, sipping carefully. I don't want to cough and alert Barney, because she's obviously never had this stuff before. I hold my breath while she lifts her bottle to her lips.

She drinks. Her eyes bulge and she stares at the bottle in her hand. "What's in this thing?"

"Yah mon. It burns a little," I say, imitating an island accent.

"A little?" Her eyes water.

I throw back my head and laugh. Ginger beer is heavy on the ginger and pepper and bites your throat all the way down. If they added alcohol to the mix, the combo would destroy a sailor.

"Guess they didn't have down-home food and drink in the fancy neighborhood you came from."

"My mother was the world's best cook, so I had no reason to go chasing after places like this before she died. I've heard about patties from an aunt who moved to Jamaica a few years ago, but she forgot to mention ginger beer." She takes a bite of the flaky brown pastry covering the meat and wipes the juices from her mouth with the back of her hand. "My aunt was right—this is good, but there must be about ten zillion calories inside this thing."

"Why is that a problem?"

"Why? You can tell I eat too much. Just look at me."

I make good use of the excuse to stare at the way she fills out her clothes. She's got smoother curves than Lake Shore Drive. I like that. Nicole and her besties act like skinny is the only way to be popular, but I like the Queen Latifah look.

Barney takes another bite, then puts her pattie down and wipes the juices from her mouth with a napkin. "I thought about you again last night." When I grin she adds, "Get that dopey smile off your face. It's only because of everything that happened, and it was more of a nightmare than anything."

My smile isn't dopey; I just can't believe she spends her nights thinking about me. I can't stop looking at her. Smooth and brown with a sheen of sweat on her face. I squirm in my seat and slip my wraparound sunglasses over my eyes to hide my stare.

"Those glasses are creepy." Her eyes narrow. I know she's trying to see through her own reflection in the dark lenses and find me.

"I wear the shades to protect my eyes," I say, and take another drink.

"I thought you were just being shy."

Ginger beer spews from my nose. "Shy?"

She squeaks, then laughs, grabs a napkin and dabs at my face. "Wrong word, huh?"

"I'm never shy." Call me overbearing. Obstinate. Badass.

Fat douchebag coward.

Shut the fuck up, Perry, my mind screams. *You're dead.*

The music changes to a song with a quick, happy beat.

"That's Enemies of Blood and Flesh," Barney says.

"Do you like their music?"

She nods. "Sometimes their stuff is a little depressing, but this song is awesome. And Horst is like...like, huge. He's like, totally cracked." She wiggles in her seat.

I hate Horst.

"They're playing at Ageless Encounters next weekend," I say. "I can get you in. Backstage passes, too." I'm insane. I can't risk going there again with my father on the warpath. But if Barney says yes, Uncle Leon better cough up the passes, because nothing will stop me from taking her.

"Ageless is a club," she says in a voice that could belong to my dad. "It's for adults. I can't get inside."

"I can get us in," I insist.

"Is that where you take all your girls?"

"I never—" I stop and lean back in my chair. I lift my bottle of ginger beer to keep from admitting she's the first girl I ever asked. The ginger tickles my nose and throat as I drain the last drops from the bottle. I need something stronger. "I need a drink."

"Here, have mine." She pushes her bottle toward me.

"No. I need the real stuff."

"You can't drink. You're not twenty-one."

"I heard you were supposed to be smart. Everyone drinks." Everyone except my dad. Even her beloved Saint David. Alcohol is natural. It's in the Torah and the Bible. Uncle Leon can down half a dozen drinks before he even begins to act drunk. Cousin John has two, maybe three, no problem. Granddad can handle as much booze as you throw at him. Even Mom has a little wine once in a while, and nothing ever happens with her. Only my dad acts like alcohol is all seven deadly sins wrapped together.

"I don't drink," Barney says. "And I don't like people who do. If you drink, I guess that explains things."

"Explains what?"

"Why you're so changeable. David thought I was crazy when I tried to tell him that you were sometimes nice. He said you were like a chair with a wobbly leg."

"Meaning?"

"That you might look reliable, but people who trust you need to expect that you'll let them down. Hard." She leans across the table, snatches the sunglasses from my face, and stares. "I thought your eyes looked strange. Are you drunk now?"

"No." Hungover and growing angry, but definitely not drunk.

"Did you play basketball drunk?"

"No way!"

"Because of drug tests?"

"Because when I play I feel..." I search for the right words to explain what being on the basketball court does for me. "A game is all the high I need. But games don't last forever, and then there's life and all the crap that goes with it."

"You drink to push away the crap?"

"Yes." I nod, glad she understands. When life gets bad, I take a drink and forget. I have lots of things I need to forget. Like how I got stupid and messed up my chances with this girl.

CHAPTER 24

There are about a million ways I'd like to spend New Year's Day. Most of them involve Barney. I arrive at Frank's and look around for her. Her boxing skills are improving, but I've decided to take on that bodyguard job.

Only someone is already there, waiting for her. Her brother, David Albacore. He must be home for the holidays. He looks older than when he left. I'd swear he's bigger, too.

Dammit.

"I understand I'm supposed to be grateful to you." David comes up to me, spitting the words like they burn his tongue.

"You weren't around when your sister needed you." The look on his face makes me feel like I've just sunk a game-winning three-pointer at the buzzer.

"I think you set up the whole thing."

"Why would I bother?"

"To be the rescuer and get back in with her. To hurt her so you can get to me again."

"I forgot about you before you even left." He thinks it's all about him. But it's about being on top. Being number one. And Barney. Mostly it's about her.

"Hey you two." Barney comes up behind him, pulling on her coat.

David whirls on her. "Seems Yolanda was right. You and this guy are together all the time."

"Your girlfriend worries too easily and tells to many tales. Malik and I are just friends."

"Barney wants to be with me," I say. Friends isn't exactly what I'm going for with the girl.

David glares at his sister. "Don't you realize Malik's a blueprint for building an idiot? If I'd thought you'd be foolish enough to let him stomp all over you again, I'd never have left."

"I'm not a fool." Her smile vanishes. "You don't really know him; he's not what you think he is."

"He's everything I think he is, and worse. You have to listen to me and stay away from him."

"I don't have to listen when you're wrong."

I can't believe how controlling she is with him. I kind of like it.

"He's just out to hurt you," David says.

"Wrong," I say. "I don't want to hurt Barney. You, I'll take on any time, any place."

"Game on," David snarls, coming so close to me his rage jumps between us like static electricity.

"No, no, no," Barney shakes her head. "This stops, now. You two can stop comparing your assets. You're both big and bad, okay?"

"I'm bigger," David says

I'm badder.

"Are you both five or something?" Barney jumps between us. She puts one hand on my chest, one on his. "If you two want to beat each other up then go out to the alley and pound away. But I won't care who wins, I don't want to see either of you again, understand? Not unless you stop this fighting. Now both of you, shake hands."

Shake hands? Now who sounds like she's five?

David stares at her. Something in his face softens. He lifts his head to meet my gaze and offers up a callused hand. "I'm willing if you are."

I don't know what to do.

"Take his hand, Malik," Barney says.

I can't move.

His hand lowers just as mine finally answers the call from my brain and begins to lift. I'm too late. I don't even think he sees.

"Let's get going." David takes Barney's hand and pulls her toward the bus stop.

"But Malik…"

"No 'buts,' Sis. Nothing changes."

He sounds tired, like Mom did when the physical therapists said they had done all they could. When she realized she would have to live with herself the way she was, forever.

"It's not about you," I say to David.

"I'm all you've ever been after," David says without turning.

"Not anymore."

"Then, why hang with my sister?" David finally turns. He frowns as if he believes.

"Yes why?" she asks. "Why were you ever interested in me?"

"Why not? The more girls the better." I can't think of anything else except to make this another joke. I can't tell him it was because of the way I felt the first time she looked at me. At me, not just how much I had in my wallet, or my car, or my point average. Just me.

"Figures." David crosses his arms over his chest.

Barney shakes her head. "I don't believe that. Tell me the truth."

I can't. Instead I turn to David and ask, "Is she always like this?"

"Mostly," he admits. "She lives to give orders."

"And you let her boss you?"

"Always."

"Why let her talk to you that way? She's a girl."

"And my sister. You should have one, then maybe you'd understand."

I think I do understand. David Albacore is intense, but he isn't cruel, crazy, or mean. He just hates me and wants to protect Barney.

I guess that's what real brothers do.

CHAPTER 25

New Years brings us back to school and the return of normal. Including second period History. The teacher, Mrs. Templin, wanders between the rows of desks, handing papers back to students. Her rubber-soled shoes produce a whispery sound that makes it easy to think of her as a ghost.

She drops a paper on Cesare's desk. He picks it up and smiles. When she reaches my desk, she pauses. Most teachers look through me. Not Mrs. Templin. She has been giving me cold stares ever since the beginning of the semester. The one she throws my way now would make penguins shiver.

She went to school with my parents. She was one of the people who grew up in the neighborhood, escaped, and then came back for some reason. Guess she couldn't make a real life for herself anywhere else. After almost a minute, she continues down the row without leaving a paper on my desk.

People rush for the door when the bell rings.

I never rush. That's how she gets me.

"I need to talk to you, Malik," she says.

Cesare stops by the door and stares back at me for a second, his face tight and unreadable. Then he shrugs and leaves the room. I take my time approaching her desk. I'm not surprised to see my test paper lying in front of her, and I'm even less surprised by the red D-minus scrawled at the top.

She massages her temple with her fingers. "Being this bad must be exhausting."

I passed, didn't I?

She taps a finger on the paper. "You left no room for error. You put in exactly the minimum, just enough to keep from failing. What happens if you miss? You were only two points from an F."

Two points? Damn, I was going for one. "I never miss."

"Do you want to know what I think?" she asks.

"Not really."

"I think you get exactly the grade you want. You were one of my best students with a solid B-plus average when you were on the team. The minute you quit basketball, you plunged to the bottom."

"I never quit."

"You chose the actions that cost you a spot on the team. You're smart enough to understand consequences. Or…maybe not. You wouldn't be the first man in your family to think life owed you a set of get out of jail free cards."

"I passed." *What is her beef?* I hate people all up in my business. She needs to leave the messing with my head stuff to Kasili.

"This isn't a game; this is your life," she says. "I thought you were planning on college. What if you fail and don't graduate?"

"Guess I'll be working in one of my dad's shops."

"An auto mechanic?" She shakes her head. "When you could use that brain of yours to design new and better engines? I thought you planned on becoming a super engineer. What happened to your dream of building the perfect hybrid car?"

"That was a joke. I was a dumbass freshman." I relaxed with her once when I found her stranded in the parking lot. Her car wouldn't start. I got it running and made the mistake of talking about engines, forgetting she was a woman and a teacher. I talked about car design, engineering, and building vehicles that run faster, that are both beautiful and safe. I know I could be the best engineer in Chicago, in the entire state, maybe the country. That's my dream, the one no one wants to hear. Perry used to say I didn't have a future. Mom says become the lawyer Dad couldn't. Dad just tells me to stay out of the shop.

"What you told me back then didn't sound like a joke," Mrs. Templin says. "Your ideas impressed me."

"Because I fixed your car?"

"Because you had plans for your future. You reminded me of your mother, before…"

Before Dad trapped her.

I can't take any more. "I have to get to my next class. The bell is ringing."

Mrs. Templin pulls a pad from her desk and fills in a late pass. She waves it in the air, but instead of handing it to me, she says, "I went to school with your parents and your uncle. Sometimes you're so like Leon Kaplan, I almost cry."

"Were you one of his girlfriends?" Is that what this is all about?

"I had more sense than to get snared by a coward who runs from his responsibilities."

"My uncle is no coward. He was a hero in the army."

"While your father remained behind and paid the price."

"What price?"

Mrs. Templin takes a deep breath. "Do you remember your response to the World View assignment? You put solid thought into that report." She begins reciting my words. "'Dinosaurs didn't think of the future. When I look around me, I see too many people doing the same thing. If we only live for today—'"

"'We'll all die tomorrow.'" I remember exactly what I wrote.

"Too few people of any age understand how lack of action damages them and the people around them. Your uncle still doesn't get that. Leon never stopped to think about the future or the child he left behind. I've said all I had to say. Except this: your father never ran away from anything. Don't run from your problems, Malik."

I hitch my pants, crumple my test paper, and toss it in the wastebasket before cruising out the door.

Nothing makes me run anymore.

Which is how Kasili catches up with me. I see him standing in the hall fourth period. His arms are crossed over his chest and he stares at me. A flick of his chin shows he wants me. I'm used to his attitude, and decide to ignore him and leave. But I feel his eyes burning my back.

I turn to face him.

He nods. It's a small move of approval, the kind I seldom got on the basketball court or at home.

"My office," he says.

Instead of herding me into the athletics center, he "invites" me upstairs to his other office, the one in the counseling center. This office is bigger than the one in the athletics wing. There are no trophies here, just a little sign on the wall above his head with four words:

Fearful

Insecure

Neurotic

Emotional

Beneath the sign is a bookcase; education and psychology books fill the space behind its glass doors. He has a stuffed animal on his desk, along with a picture of his family.

"I don't suppose you asked me here to discuss game strategy." I sit back in the chair he points to and cross one leg over the other. I hear the motor of the clock on his desk. Snow falls outside the window. Sweat trickles down my neck as he stares at me. I remember what I disliked most about this man. He's the silent treatment king. He never yelled and rarely raised his voice, just stared at guys until they squirmed. That's how he controlled the team.

Kasili has no control over me anymore.

He lifts one hand and rubs his chin. "For what it's worth, I'm glad you're back in school. I admire the way your father handled things with the administration and got you reinstated. I wish…had it been up to me, you would still be on the team as well."

"Because you need me."

"Because *you* need the team."

"There's no way I'll ever play for you again. I hate the game." The truth is I didn't realize how much basketball meant to me until I lost the right to play.

"Maybe you do, today." He tightens his lips. "How are things at home?"

"My parents are fine."

"That's not what I asked."

It's all I'll tell him. "Mrs. Templin sent you after me, didn't she?"

"Mrs. Templin, and the vice principal."

"Oh, hell."

"You do understand you're under a microscope. Every move you make is being closely watched." His fingers drum on the desktop. The sound makes my head hurt.

"I know. Stay away from Spencer. I don't even go to the lunch-room anymore, just to keep Henderson happy. What more do you want from me?"

"Mr. Henderson thinks you and I should have regular meetings. Just to talk."

"No way. I don't need a shrink messing with my head."

"Not messing. I'd call it more like a fifty thousand mile, or seven-teen-year-old tune-up. Think of your brain as a fine car, an Infiniti."

"Mustang."

"I stand corrected." He laughs. "Even…no, especially a Mustang needs scheduled maintenance, much more than the occasional oil change. Better to have the experts go over things before there's a real problem."

"No mechanic gets to tinker under my hood."

"Needing help is not a bad thing, Malik."

"My brain is a precision machine. I don't need anything."

Kasili turns to the computer on his desk and hits a few keys. I can't see the screen, but I know he's looking at my records when he sighs. I know what he sees. Teacher's pet in grade school. Teacher's nightmare after eighth grade.

"You've troubled me from the first," Kasili says. "When you're on there's no one better, but you're as inconsistent in class as you are on the court. At times near perfect, like you don't know how to make a mistake. Then suddenly, everything reverses. You become surly, with-drawn, and you can't work with anyone. You're a mess of contradic-tions."

"Everyone knows what I am."

"Do we? Really? You've always been near the top. Three-point-eight GPA, including a number of accelerated courses in science and engineering."

"Don't forget high point-scorer on the court."

"I don't forget anything. I bet you don't either." His deep voice echoes through the room. That shrink face continues staring at me. "Did you ever see anyone after your brother died? The loss of a sibling is a major trauma."

"It was six years ago." Is that on his computer too? How much do people know?

"You're not the only one who's lost someone they love. Did you ever get any help? There are programs available for students with emotional problems."

"I have no emotional problems." I am *not* Perry. I'm not the one who drowned in his own puke.

"I understand if you don't want to talk to me." Kasili grabs a piece of paper, scribbles something, and extends it toward me. "I personally recommend this program."

Personally?

The paper I refuse to touch hangs in the air for several seconds before he lets it rest on his desk.

Why is everyone trying to send me somewhere for *help?* Kasili, Zach…they aren't me. They don't know anything about me. I'd rather deal with Henderson. I can handle a man who thinks I'm walking dirt.

I walk out, slamming the door behind me.

CHAPTER 26

When I enter Frank's Place, Barney looks up from pouring coffee for a customer and smiles. My stomach jumps. Her wide eyes almost make me forget everything. She's soft and curved in all the right places. Underneath she's plenty tough. Instead of her usual braid, her hair is loose and falls around her shoulders. I've taken on the bodyguard role. I get a free cup of coffee while I wait for her to finish her shift.

"I won't be at the Outlet on Saturday," she says, as we take our seats on the bus.

I'll miss her. I feel like I can relax and be myself when we're together. "Tired of getting squashed in the ring?"

She rolls her eyes. "You know I got through your blocks."

"You're improving, I admit it." The girl no longer throws pitty-pat punches. The power in her left jab took me by surprise the last time we sparred; she almost had me kissing the canvas. What I really want is to kiss her. I want to take care of her. To protect her. She doesn't need to fight. If anyone tried to hurt her now I would rip them apart.

"I have to visit my father this Saturday," Barney says.

"At the prison?"

She nods.

"Don't go," I say, but I know it's not always easy to do what you want.

"I have to go with my aunt. She's in a wheelchair and can't make it alone." The Enforcer couldn't make her cry, but thinking about the man who killed her mother makes her chin quiver. She brushes aside a tear with the back of one hand. "It's not so bad. It's only a couple of times a month. My father always thanks me for coming. Last time he even told me he was sorry and asked me to forgive him."

"You told him to go to hell, right?"

"Maybe I'm a better liar than I know, because when I said sure, he patted my head and nodded. I think he really believes."

"You should have told him the truth."

"That would upset my aunt. She's happy that he claims he's found God. The truth is, I don't care. Maybe he found God, or God found him, but it won't bring Mom back." She bites her bottom lip and sighs. "My aunt says forgive and forget. She loves him; he's her brother. David says to hell with him, that I don't have to forgive."

"I never thought I'd agree with your brother on anything."

Barney smiles. "I'll have to tell him a miracle occurred. "At least my father goes to Alcoholics Anonymous meetings in prison. Maybe he'll really stop drinking. Kasili's after me to start going to Alateen meetings."

"Alateen? What's that?"

"A place where I can talk about things."

It must be some kind of therapy group. Kasili leads a couple of them at school for people who want to sit around and talk about how bad life is. She doesn't need to talk to strangers. I could do more for her than any stupid group. "We should get off the bus and hustle over to the Outlet and have a round with the punching bag," I say. "That's what I'd do, get out and hurt something."

"You're not just talking about the punching bag, are you?" Her smile vanishes. "You mean hurt someone?"

"Why not, if it helps?"

"Does it really? You prowl the halls at school like G.I. Joe on combat duty. You hurt people. Does that help you? What did you feel after you beat up Spencer?"

"I don't want to talk about that."

"You don't talk much about yourself."

"I'm a private guy."

"Malik Kaplan, private? Loud parties and very public arguments. The only private things about you are your hater-blockers." Once again, she snatches away the shades shielding my face. I reach for the glasses, but she stuffs them in her pocket before asking, "In all the world, who do you hate most?"

Me, myself, and I.

"What about Yolanda?" she asks, when I don't respond. "When you treated her like a punching bag with benefits, did that make you feel good?"

That's another memory I want to forget, but at least I have an answer. "Girls sometimes forget who's in charge. You don't respect us if we let you get away with stuff." I feel my uncle's hand patting me on the back as I speak.

"And that's why you lost her."

"I lost her because of your brother."

"You drove her away. You weren't in love with her anyway."

"This isn't about Yolanda, or about love; it's about respect—something your brother tried to take from me."

"I respected you." Her voice is suddenly soft. "I liked you the first time I saw you." Something flickers in Barney's eyes as she stares at me.

I need those shades. But I'd have to touch her to get them back, and I don't dare, not now. I glance up at the roof of the bus, hoping maybe God will help me find words to explain something I don't understand myself. But my silent prayer means nothing; God sends me no help.

"I didn't mean to hurt Yolanda," I say. "I drank a little too much and lost my temper, that's all."

"That's what my father used to say." Her voice cracks. "He came home night after night, soaked in beer or wine or whiskey or whatever, and treated Mom like the heavy bag."

"Did he hurt you?"

"He killed my mother." She sniffles and rubs tears from her cheeks. "If you want to know if he ever hit me, then no. Maybe that's why I never said or did anything when he went after her. I was afraid he would turn on me. I was happy when she divorced him. Until the night he came back and shot her. When she died, I wanted to die too."

"Barney." I reach for her hands. She doesn't pull away until I touch her wristbands, the ones that hide the scars left when she tried to kill herself.

"When my father got drunk, he got cruel and stopped caring about any of us, including his big old horse of a daughter."

"If that's what he thought of you, he was wrong."

"It's what *you* thought. Big old horse who doesn't matter, so you could laugh at me, pull me down, use me…"

I was wrong. "You matter." I understand now why her brother was willing to give up so much for her. Everything about Barney turns me on. How did I let this girl get away?

"Hater-blockers." She pulls out my glasses and tosses them at me. "I guess you need these." As the bus pulls up to her stop, she climbs to her feet. "You could be so much *more* if you didn't drink."

"What if I stop drinking? Could you like me then?" Tension builds in the air between me and Barney.

"Can you stop?" she asks.

Easy-peasy. I control my life and I live for challenges. I snap my fingers. "No problem."

CHAPTER 27

Let's be smart and blow this place." Cesare's lips tighten as he looks over the abandoned three-flat apartment building. Graffiti decorates the front door, the porch sags, and the windows are boarded up. "This place is abandoned. And it should be condemned."

"What, you scared?" I ask.

"I just don't see a reason to be stupid."

"This is the right address." But I almost wish Cesare hadn't said anything. His words mean I can't leave without looking like a coward. The lock is broken; the door swings open when I touch it. Rats scurry in the darkness as we climb to the third-floor apartment. The smell of alcohol and weed fills the air.

Lamont's eyes narrow when Cesare enters after me. "What's he doing here?"

"He's with me," I say.

Lamont hesitates only a second before nodding at Cesare. "I remember you."

"Couldn't forget you, either," Cesare says.

There are three other guys in the room, including Dreadlocks. He recognizes me, too. His lips twist into the kind of smile an exterminator uses while laying out rat poison.

"Malik, you look like a man in need of a drink." Lamont lifts a hand and the older guy freezes. Obviously he's just muscle. Easy to tell who's in charge. "Darnell, go get a bottle of gin, and three glasses."

"Only three?" Dreadlocks' eyes narrow.

"Don't question me, just do what I told you."

There's no respect in the look Dreadlocks throws at Lamont before leaving the room.

The room is filled with the kind of furniture even scrap scavengers might leave behind. But these guys have their own place and live like they want. No one tells them what to do. Lamont stands by a small round table with two chairs. He points me at one and sits in the other. Cesare grabs a crate and sits beside me.

"Your guy doesn't look too happy," I say.

"Darnell and I hooked up a little while ago," Lamont says. He taps his head. "The old guy is strong as a bulldog and about as brainless. People used to listen to him, but he kept screwing up. But he keeps thinking he should be boss because he's older."

Darnell returns with a bottle and glasses that he sets nosily on the table. His glare at Lamont shows he's not deaf. I don't see how Lamont ever turns his back on the guy.

"Now get lost until I call you," Lamont says. "All of you. I'm having a private conversation with my new friends."

"Are you guys the only squatters in this building?" Cesare asks when we're alone.

"The only ones that count." Lamont fills the glasses and hands one to me. He extends the other to Cesare, who shakes his head and frowns.

"What are you doing around here?" Cesare asks.

"We lived in Uptown, but then Moms lost her job and moved into that shelter. I came with her and Darnell followed me. I think I like this area—you've got a sweet neighborhood, Malik. I'm thinking maybe I'll hang here for a while."

"That could cause trouble," Cesare says.

"I don't run from trouble." Lamont turns from Cesare to me, obviously annoyed by all of his questions. "The old guys have grown soft. I'm going to turn back time and bring the Enforcers back to the top, the way things are supposed to be. You're into all that school stuff; I bet you know about the men in history who changed their world. Great men like William the Bastard, Alexander the Great, Conan."

"The talk show guy?" Cesare asks with a puzzled frown.

I feel as confused as he sounds. That doesn't fit.

"No, dude, the barbarian." Disgust fills Lamont's deep voice. He

there isn't anything we couldn't have."

"Why me? You have plenty of guys. Guys like Darnell."

"I have dozens like Darnell," Lamont says. "He's not too bright or the kind who can lead, and he wouldn't last long alone. I think big and plan bigger. You're my kind of people. You and me, what do you think?"

I think this is my chance to prove Perry was wrong about me. I spent years trying to prove I didn't need him, didn't need anyone. I made myself the best at everything that counted. But it never felt like enough. I take another drink, feel the warmth spread through my body. This stuff is smooth, and way better than beer. I'll probably never settle for beer again.

"If I agree, then Cesare comes too," I say.

"No way. He wouldn't fit in." Lamont falls back into his chair and shakes his head.

"He fits with me. Both of us, or neither of us." Someone wants me, and I don't know why I hesitate. It's hard to think, but I know I can't desert Cesare.

A flash of anger jumps from Lamont's eyes. Then he leans back and picks up the bottle. He refills my glass, then tosses the now empty bottle in a pile of trash in one corner. A rat squeals as the pile shifts.

"No problem," Lamont says. "We'll talk again. If your boy wants to be one of us, bring him along."

CHAPTER 28

When Cesare and I became friends, so did our fathers. Once our families went on picnics together and our fathers even joined the same bowling league. All that ended by the time Cesare and I entered seventh grade. When the Russos got behind on their mortgage, the bank foreclosed. Dad bought their house from the bank. Then he also bought the house next door, had both torn down, and built his McMansion on the two lots.

Cesare and I fought, repeating words we barely understood:

"My dad says your dad's screwing us over."

"My dad says your dad's a freeloader."

But what Cesare and I had didn't die when our parents became enemies. He and I got over things. Maybe the priests and rabbis really are onto something, because even God didn't take him from me. Without a God, how could the two of us have been among the few who survived the bus crash and fire that killed the old coach and most of last year's team? Cesare was too sick to go to that away game. I fought with the coach and refused to ride the team bus that night.

"Why'd you just walk out like that?" I ask, when I catch up to my friend. "What was your problem?" My tongue feels thick, my words come out slowly. I stop and shake my head, trying to clear my thoughts.

"My problem?" He stops in the middle of the sidewalk, cheeks flushed from the January cold. "That Lamont dude's crap about me not belonging. And you didn't say a word to stop him."

"Doesn't matter now." I shake my head again. I don't remember much of what Lamont said to Cesare. Why is this so hard? "He wants me to join. No, us. He wants us to join."

"It's a dead-end road. I don't want that and neither do you."

"Don't tell me what I want."

"Go ahead, join that band of try-hard losers if you want, but leave me out."

"I fought for you." How freaking dare he stand there giving me a superior look? My head throbs, my stomach clutches, and I don't even know why I left Lamont or his endless supply of gin.

"You're drunk again." Cesare sounds disgusted. "Haven't we had enough trouble?"

"We? I'm the one who had a power-tripping judge jumping down my throat. The guy talked down to me like I was next in line for death row. Did you even care what I went through? Or were you too busy laughing because my ass was the only one hanging in the wind?"

"I never laughed at you. I know what I owe you." He slaps his head and groans. "I should tell people what really happened, only that would kill my old man. It was just one toke. Why the hell did I let Spencer get to me? But he insulted my girl."

"Keep acting sappy and Giselle will never respect you." I don't want to hear about him and his girl again.

"You don't know anything about Giselle and me."

"I know she stomps all over you because you're too stupid to know how to handle her. I know Nicole did a better job educating her sister than I did training you. Let me tell you something about the Mitchell sisters. They only value men who demand respect."

"Giselle isn't like her sister."

"She's exactly like her. And soon she'll push you aside the way you're doing to me."

Cesare reaches for me.

"Keep your distance, Russo. Remember what *daddy* said about me."

He flinches. "I'm not tossing you aside, we're still friends..."

"Screw friendship. Respect is what matters. Do you respect me?"

He takes a deep breath and says, "What do you want, my friendship or my respect?"

"Both." Friendship can't be trusted. Even my family betrays me. I have to be safe. I must have respect.

"Pick one. You have to choose."

Choose? I can barely think. "Respect."

Emotions race across Cesare's face: anger, confusion, hatred, fear...pain. His eyes close for a moment, as if he can't believe what he heard. Then he gives a tight nod. "Fine. You want respect, you got it. And that's all you get from me from now on, Kaplan."

It's what I need, and I won't let myself want anything more. Not from anyone.

Back when our parents became enemies, I asked Cesare why he stayed with me. "You're my friend," he answered back then. "I don't abandon you."

That was then, and this is now. Now he looks at me like an old zoo tiger being led around by the trainer and his whip. He shrugs and walks away. My head whirls and aches. My heart pumps hard and fast, as if Cesare and I had been in a fight.

No fight. We just aren't friends anymore.

I pull the Christmas present he gave me from my pocket. The words on page sixty-nine dance.

...feeling powerless is an occasional and unfortunate fact of life.

Not for me. This isn't me. I will not let this be my life.

I tear the book in half and toss the pages into the street.

*

"If these things don't kill me the cold will, but I can't give them up," Dad says. He stands in a shadow at one end of the porch. I see the light glowing at the tip of his cigar and smell an aroma that reminds me of being little and following him around, crawling under cars and pretending I knew enough to help. Days when I was young and stupid and wanted to be like him.

His hand lifts. Red and yellow light flares. He blows out a perfect smoke ring.

Dad loves his cigars. Mom doesn't and forbids smoking inside the house. I've seen him stand out here in a blizzard. Maybe, after all these years of living together, what's between my parents has grown into something more than just a have-to marriage. Maybe how things start doesn't matter as much as how they end.

A delivery truck rattles down the street. I think about Cesare and his father. Dad and Mr. Russo used to be friends. Maybe not super close like me and Cesare. Not closer than brothers—someone you could trust with anything. But still, I wonder if Dad felt like his guts were being yanked from his throat when he and Mr. Russo pulled apart?

"What happened between us and the Russo family?" I ask.

"Money." The word explodes into the cold air. "The root of all evil," Dad continues in a softer voice. "Of broken friendships, anyway."

"He blames you for losing his house."

"I know. When I bought the place from the bank, I also found myself owning a new enemy with a gut full of hatred. I guess it makes him feel better to think I took something from him."

"You could have given him what he needed. He was your friend."

"You think I should give money away?" Dad shakes his head. "No one ever gave me anything."

"Mom did."

He coughs like I sucker-punched him in the stomach. "Your mother and I are a team. I can never repay what I owe her. And I don't want people to feel they owe me." He sighs and rubs the back of his neck with one hand. "Maybe I should have handed out the Chanukah *gelt* just that once, given Brian what he needed, hoped he wouldn't gamble that away, too. I sometimes look back and wish I'd done things differently, but the past can't be changed." Dad's fist pounds the porch railing. "Some endeavors deserve to fail. Sometimes people are better for it. It's about drive and independence and the future. The pain of failure enables us to remember and profit from our mistakes. It's cruel, but there's really no choice—that's how human beings learn."

Learn what? Don't help your friend?

"I get that someone had to be punished for what happened at Spencer's house," I say. "I get the stupid essay, even the community service. But the judge never said anything about me and basketball; what was I supposed to learn from getting kicked off the team?"

"I didn't know they were going to do that," Dad says gruffly.

"Could you get me back on the squad?" I say.

"I'm sorry, no."

"You got me back in school."

"That was different."

"How?"

He stares off into the sky as if listening to some inner voice. "If I jumped in to save you, paid your fine and got you back on the basketball team, what would you have learned?"

He rescued Perry all the time. What did my brother learn?

"Is that why you won't help Granddad get back his license?"

"My father needs much more help than I can give." The glasses come off again.

"Because of one accident? OK, so he had a drink—"

"Not *a* drink. He's an alcoholic. He got drunk and got behind the wheel and almost killed someone. He's a danger to himself and to others."

"Why don't you at least let him live with us?"

"Because I'm no longer a masochist. I won't just give, not for him or anyone else. Not even kids really like Santa; they just expect presents. Adults start expecting rescue. Why try too hard when you can sit back and gather handouts and then learn to hate your benefactor when the gifts stop coming." His lips press tight, eyes seem to focus inward. "Some endeavors deserve to fail, Malik. Sometimes people are better for it."

"Not always."

"Maybe not, but I'm not the man to pick and choose."

"You just pick up pieces after things fall. Is that why you keep buying buildings, adding to your collection?"

"Is that a bad thing?" He grunts. "Let's say a business fails and leaves a building abandoned. What happens then? Another drug hangout and haven for lowlifes."

Dad's glasses come off again. He rubs his eyes and stares at me. "This is about your car, isn't it? You think you can talk me into giving it back. You won't succeed."

Just like that, the closeness is gone, and we're back to the way we've always been. He sighs and walks into the house.

I had totally forgotten about my car.

CHAPTER 29

Y
o, Connie," I say when I stop by the shelter's office to check in. I'm two hours early, but I want to take the kid out for breakfast.

"You appear to be in a hurry to get rid of us." Connie no longer tries to correct me about her name. She leans back in her chair and smiles.

"What do you mean?" I like this place. I even like her.

"You're here so often, racking up the hours, your sentence will be over soon."

Now that winter break has begun, I'm here almost every day. What else is there to do?

T'Shawn and I go to Frank's Place. I know Barney doesn't work in the mornings, but I'm still disappointed that a stranger takes my breakfast order. T'Shawn barely looks up from my phone and the game he's playing when she comes to the table.

"Hey, Short-stack." The speaker stands just inside the door. His face is in shadow, backlit from the sunlight streaming through the windows, but I instantly recognize the gravel-filled voice and bald head. It's been weeks since we shared a jail, but I haven't forgotten the Enforcer.

"Lamont!" T'Shawn tosses my phone on the table and jumps from his seat. His chair crashes to the floor as he runs across the restaurant. He grabs the Enforcer's hand and pulls him back to our table.

"So, you're the guy Wiggins sicced on T," the Enforcer says.

"I'm the guy," I say calmly.

"This is Malik," T'Shawn says. "He's my friend."

"And you're Lamont," I say. "T'Shawn won't stop talking about you."

He smiles, tight and proud. I see the resemblance; if he had a little hair he'd be a bigger, taller version of T'Shawn.

"Did you know the cops are scared of Malik?" T'Shawn says.

"Are they?" Lamont stares at me. The smile fades; his face is back to all business. I see why Connie wouldn't let him in the shelter. Not just the age. His attitude is cold. He's not the kind of guy to follow rules. I stand to take full advantage of my superior height. If he wants to start something, I'm ready.

Frank comes running from the back. "I told you never to come in my place again."

Lamont rolls his eyes. "I come in peace and all that crap. Why you want to make trouble, old man?"

"I've seen more trouble than you could dream of." Frank's voice is cold and steady. "What I don't want is you hanging around my place."

"I'm here to see my little brother and eat a little something, that's all. It's a free country, man."

"Not inside my restaurant. Eat elsewhere. I don't want to see your face here again."

Lamont's hand slips into his pocket. I can imagine what he'll pull out.

"This isn't the place for a fight," I say.

He glances around. The restaurant is packed. People are staring. One man at a nearby table is already on his feet, as if he intends to band together with Frank. An elderly couple sits motionless, except for the cellphone in the woman's hand. The camera is aimed in our direction.

Lamont shrugs. "You don't want my business, that's your loss," he tells Frank. Then he grabs a napkin from the table, pulls out a pen, and scribbles something.

"Loyalty is the rarest thing in the world," Lamont says as he writes. "It's precious and deserves to be rewarded. That's why I have an offer for you."

"What kind of offer?"

"Come see me." He stuffs the napkin in my pocket, cuffs T'Shawn on the side of the head, and leaves. He moves with that lean in his walk, the one designed to tell people he's in total control.

Frank glares at me, as if he thinks I belong with the gang and wants to order me off his property too. Then he shakes his head and goes back to the kitchen.

"You need to be careful with Lamont," I tell T'Shawn. "He could get you thrown out of the shelter."

"I don't care. I don't need that place. I want to live with Lamont."

"You don't really think he wants you to stay with him, do you?"

"Of course he does. He says we're a set, we're supposed to be together. He says that's what makes me a good brother—I'm useful to him."

*

"Do I mean anything to you?" I ask my granddad. My arm aches from the blow I had to take as the price of admittance to his apartment. My jacket hangs on the back of the chair John usually sits in. He refused to come tonight.

Granddad's brow furrows. "Don't I always say you're my favorite grandson?"

Because I let him win our senseless battles? Because I keep him company when he has no one else?

Because I'm a drinking buddy?

He puts a beer in front of me.

"I don't feel like drinking tonight," I say.

"It's not poison."

My heart beats faster and my tongue grows thick, but I tell him, "It's just that I promised Barney I'd stop drinking."

Granddad starts and then blinks several times. I think he's trying to keep my face in focus as he says, "Then don't tell him."

"Not him. Barney's a girl."

"Oh Lord, are you gonna let a woman rule you the way Celeste does Dwayne?" He shakes his head and pops open his own can. After taking a swallow he belches. "Dwayne was a surly kid, a wuss who used to cower in his room, nose stuck in some book on account of being too scared to get out like a real man and face the world."

But I like Barney. She doesn't try to rule me. She listens to what I say. And when I don't want to talk, she's okay with that too. Maybe she's not one of the hot girls, but she is the one I want to be with.

He drinks, crushes his can and tosses it at the wastebasket. It misses and bounces on the floor as he returns to the fridge and brings back two more cans. He tries again to hand me another beer.

"I haven't even started this one," I protest, but he doesn't listen and I don't fight when he places the second can beside the first. I stare at the beers I want and don't want at the same time. My heart beats three strong thumps. My tongue grows thick. I close my hand around the beer can, feel the cold wetness on my palm from the perspiring glass. I swear I hear the drink call me.

Drink me. I'll get you to the place where nothing matters.

I want a drink, I don't want it. Like those "she loves me, she loves me not," games, where you know from the start how things will end, but you still have to play.

Maybe just one. Just to take the edge off.

The door opens. My father enters the apartment. His coat is unbuttoned. He's not even wearing a tie.

Granddad's eyes narrow. "Dwayne. I thought you said you'd never darken my doorstep again."

"I'm here for my son." Dad looks at me, then at the beer cans in front of me. "If he's caught with alcohol…"

"He's inside my place. How's he gonna get caught, unless you plan on turning your own kid in? Of course, you might. You let that little snitch lie and parade a few bruises to turn everyone against your own flesh and blood."

My father turns to me. "Did Spencer lie?" It almost sounds like he wants me to say yes, but I stay silent. My lies bind my lips. I still can't rat on Cesare.

Dad grabs my jacket and throws it at me. "Let's go."

I bundle the jacket in my arms and head for the door. I know what my dad is thinking. Someday this will be the two of us. That's the way my family works. And what real man wants to live like this?

"How can you be like that to your own father? You say respect your elders, you say—"

"I say people need to earn respect. Something I learned from him." He points at his father. "When people drag you down, they need to be cut from your life."

He's a jellyfish all right. And his stingers have real poison.

CHAPTER 30

I managed to pick up a few extra hours without taking over Wanda's position, even though my new job means driving the tow truck that brings Mr. Henderson's stalled car into the repair bay. It's almost closing time. Most of the mechanics are preparing to leave, so I start checking for the problem. The car looks good: flashy, fancy grill, custom interior, but one look under the hood shows the problem. Vice Principal Henderson, paces around, looking nervous as I hook up the diagnostic equipment. He apparently doesn't get the meaning of the words "oil change" or "regular maintenance." The engine is so clogged it makes Cousin John's dinosaur look healthy.

"You can get it going again, can't you?" Henderson talks fast, but the anxious note in his voice shows he knows the car is toast.

"You need a new engine. This disaster deserves a decent burial," I say. Wanda would probably frown and lecture me on tact again, but this long-suffering machine deserves someone who'll stick up for it.

Dad comes out of his office. Henderson walks over to him. "Dwayne, get me a real mechanic. I need my car. Just tell me how much it will cost to get things fixed."

I see wheels turning in Dad's head. We could have someone patch this thing and let it limp a little longer, but it won't be worth the time or money. Only you don't say things like that to people too dumb to hear the truth. Not when they have the money to pay for worthless repairs. Henderson is as bad as my mother's brothers. They can't even change the oil in their own cars, and one once asked me if a hemi was a disease.

"Malik may be young," Dad says, "but he is a real mechanic. One of my best."

"If he's your best, maybe I should take my business elsewhere." Henderson's jowls shake.

"That's your right. I'll arrange to have the car towed to any other shop you want. No charge. But it's a waste of your time and money."

"You should listen," I say. "Keep asking around and you'll find someone to take your money, but no one does a better job than we do. If a man tries to be honest with you, you should be smart and listen."

Dad places a hand on my shoulder and says, "Could you go upstairs and handle the office for a few minutes?"

Henderson is a big guy. I step close to Dad and whisper, "You might need me."

"I won't," Dad says. He's not dissing me, I realize. He's saying he has control of the situation. He knows he's right and is determined not to fight. No fists or curses. He's just a better man than Henderson.

I reach the top of the stairs and hesitate outside the office door. I look down and watch Henderson.

"I warned you about buying this car," Dad says. "The prior owners never kept up basic maintenance. You're wasting even more money trying to fix it one problem at a time. If you want to get someone else to look at it, I can't stop you. But this vehicle is way past the point of being an unstoppable money pit. You have to stop patching. You need a new engine, so you don't find yourself standing by the side of the road some freezing winter night. Better still, you need a new car."

"And I suppose you'll sell me one?"

"Chicago has plenty of car dealerships." Dad stands calm, a lion tamer with no need for a whip. Henderson laughs. Dad nods and puts a hand on his shoulder.

I've seen Dad do it before. Customers and competitors come in angry and leave as his best friend.

I enter the office and drop into Dad's black leather chair. I begin looking at the pictures on his desk. Pictures of Mom and me. And Perry. My perfect brother stares back at me: Perry at ages ten, twelve, fifteen, and eighteen.

I reach for Dad's computer keyboard. Another minute and I discover that his online life is as boring as his real life.

First, there's the security. It's nonexistent. I'm an athlete, not a hacker, but I only need a few keystrokes to learn that the password here is the same one he uses at home. The one I figured out in tenth grade.

"What are you thinking, old man?" I mutter, as I browse through his files. Probably that not many people are out to steal the secrets of an auto repair shop. The machine is six years old and slow. Virus protection, but no firewall. I should fix that for him. There are no cookies to porn sites, or email exchanges with a mystery woman.

But there are pictures. Video clips too.

I start one up. It's from one of my games. The camera remains focused on me, catching my drive down the court for a lay-up. Did Dad take these? If he videotaped my games, why didn't he ever come up to me and say something once the game ended?

I close the video and look closer at an open Word document. It's a letter to Alderman Whyte. The first line jumps at me: *I deeply regret having to turn down your nomination to the Urban Management Committee...*

He says he doesn't feel qualified.

WTF?

That's a load of bull. When a captain chooses players and picks you first, you're supposed to strut. That means you're the best, the first-round pick, the superstar. Dad should accept props for that. How can he say he's not qualified?

Because of me?

Just yesterday, the mayor dismissed someone because of "alleged improprieties" by his brother-in-law. That means he did something and got caught. A son must be worse. If I had known how much my lie would hurt Dad, I might have made a different decision that night.

I hear a cough from the open door. Dad stands watching me.

"Why are you turning the alderman down?" I stand and walk around the desk.

"You saw?" His eyes flicker from the computer to me. He looks calm but I hear strain in his voice.

"Well, yeah." Why pretend I didn't spy on him?

"I should have guessed you'd get into the system." He coughs again.

"It's because of me, isn't it? My being me messes things up for your business."

"My business and personal lives are completely separate. I simply don't have the qualifications to be an effective member of the committee. " He shakes his head, as if trying to push down some pain.

"Because you're not a lawyer? You've done a lot. Why pretend you can't do more?"

"I've kept some abandoned properties from becoming derelict, that's all. A drop in the bucket compared to what is needed." He shoves his glasses up on his forehead and wipes his eyes.

"You could get them to stop closing businesses and taking people's houses."

"I wish it were that simple."

"It should be."

He shakes his head. "The foreclosures are only a symptom. Without money, the businesses fail. The buildings aren't kept up, repairs aren't made, places fall derelict. You tell me, is that really better?"

CHAPTER 31

T'Shawn and I chose to ignore the cold and hike by the Museum of Science and Industry. Our steps echo against the stone walls as we walk through the pedestrian underpass underneath Lake Shore Drive. The roof rattles, shaken by the flow of cars and buses overhead.

We emerge near the beach. Across the waves, the dark outline of a boat marks the point where water and sky meet. Gulls dive through the air with loud squawks and land on the waves. In the distance I see a jogger, a figure in yellow and black that pulls my eyes. Someone whizzes past on the bike path. An old man walks slowly with a small dog on a leash. He nods as he passes.

"Lamont wanted me to go with him." T'Shawn won't stop talking about his brother. "Lamont Says" should be the kid's nickname. "Lamont says he's blowing this city real soon."

"Do you really want to leave your mother?" I ask. "And your sister?"

He kicks a mound of snow. "I don't know. She's so little, I guess she has to stay. But I hate being in that shelter. Lamont says I need to stay ready to roll when the time's right. I gotta do what he tells me to do."

"No, you don't."

He picks up a rock and throws as hard as he can. It hits the side of a half-submerged boulder with a loud clang. "What do you care? The minute your sentence is over you'll be gone. And what are *you* staring at?"

"I didn't mean to stare." Barney's voice comes from behind me.

I turn my head. She wears a yellow jacket, unzipped to show a tight black sweater and black sweatpants. Her hair is tied in a ponytail draped down her back. A little sheen of sweat covers her cheeks.

"You said to run every other day. I put in twenty minutes of upper body work too." She lifts her arms and strikes a body-builder pose. "I think my muscles are growing."

Her upper body is just fine. The muscles are nice, too.

"Go away. We don't need no girls," T'Shawn says. His annoyed snort makes me smile. Someday girls will be one of the things he only used to hate.

Barney climbs on a narrow stone ledge about waist high, and begins walking, slowly, arms outstretched to keep her balance. Her cheeks glow. I clap. She does a pirouette before jumping off.

"Ladies and gentlemen, a perfect ten to Murhaselt on the balance beam." I bow.

"You're silly," she says.

She's perfect.

"I can do that, too," T'Shawn says. He climbs the fence and begins walking. Barney watches him and smiles. I fight the urge to jump up there with him and show her what I can do.

When he descends, T'Shawn tugs at my jacket. "Is she your girlfriend?" he asks in a whisper so loud even the gulls must hear him.

I turn to Barney. "What do you say?" *Yes; please say yes.*

Her lips tighten for a moment before she shakes her head. "No, Malik and I are just friends."

"Friends?" *WTF?* Why can't we be more? I did what she wanted. Maybe "no problem" was an exaggeration. There were times in the last week when I would have just about killed for a beer. But I've stayed sober. If I don't count drinking with Lamont. Or the visits with my granddad.

Those were obligations. They can't count. Besides, no one caught me; I didn't get into any trouble.

I can get her to want me. I did it once, I can do it again. How hard can it be? I only have to look at my mother to know that girls will forgive almost anything.

T'Shawn continues playing on the fence. I lean closer to Barney. She doesn't pull away. I kiss her. She's soft and warm and for a second my mind goes blank.

She pushes me away and steps back.

"Why did you do that?" She wipes her mouth with a shaky hand.

I don't know what to say. I grin before shrugging and turning away. At least she didn't hit me. Good thing, since her left cross has improved.

"You won't even let me be nice to you," she says.

"That's why."

"Why what?"

"Why I kissed you. Because you've been nice to me. And you're here."

"I'm here and Nicole isn't, so you just grab me and kiss me? Without my permission and without an apology?"

"I said I was sorry."

"You never did."

"Did too."

"Did not. You just grinned, turned your head, and shrugged." She pauses. "Was that supposed to be boyspeak for sorry?"

"No. Yes." What's wrong with me? I like her. Why doesn't she feel what I feel, what I want?

"Julian Morales," I say.

"What about him?" She blinks and looks puzzled.

"He's your boyfriend, isn't he?"

"He's my friend, that's all. I don't have a boyfriend. But you do have a girlfriend."

That ends. Now.

Nicole is history. At least saying goodbye to that girl really will be easy-peasy.

*

"We need to talk," I tell Nicole the next day, when I find her coming out of the nurse's office. She has a bundle of papers in her hands. The red stripe in her hair is like a beacon. I ignore her scowl. I could have dropped her by text, but that feels cowardly. I'll just tell Nicole we're done. We've moved apart. Things haven't been the same between us in a long time so I figure the odds of an explosion are less than fifty-fifty.

"Oh, so now you need to talk," she says. "Well, so do I." She shifts the papers in her hands and looks around, almost like she's looking for help, before saying, "I'm tired of being a nobody's girl."

"I'll never be a nobody." My fingers curl into fists so tight my nails dig into my palms.

"You can't do anything for me anymore; you can't even do much for yourself. That's why I'm breaking up with you. We're over."

What's going on?

She's dropping *me*?

"It's just…I have to think about the future. Don't think this is easy for me, but it's not just about the two of us anymore." Her face twists, likes she's about to throw up.

At least it's over. I got what I wanted. Only this feels wrong. Like someone has thrust a knife between my ribs and twisted it and the blood is draining from my chest.

A paper falls from her hands as she leaves. I pick it up and see one of the nurse's brochures. There's a picture of a girl on the cover, a pregnant girl. The title reads *Your Baby's Future*.

Everything changes when one plus one makes three.

Weight gain, sour moods, clingy attitude.

Malik plus Nicole made three.

My chest tightens. The air grows so heavy, I feel like I'm drowning. Nicole has to think about something—someone—more. Just like Wanda.

Nicole is pregnant. She's having a baby.

My baby.

CHAPTER 32

My uncle's dark, unshaven fills the front door. He has a heavily wrinkled shopping bag under one arm. In spite of the chilly air, sweat covers his forehead.

"What are you doing here?" I look over his shoulder at the driveway. His car is parked half-on, half-off the snow-covered lawn. "Aren't you supposed to be at work?"

He frowns so hard I almost feel his brain struggle. "As a matter of fact, no. I am once again between jobs."

Even for him this is a record.

"Go home," I say.

He lets out a heavy sigh and shakes his head. "Don't have one of those anymore either. Let me in. Just for tonight."

"You know what my parents will say." But he's my uncle. He's family. I can't abandon another member of my family.

"Don't tell my brother."

I glance at the kitchen door. The smell of fried chicken fills the room. Mom's inside fixing dinner. Dad will be home any minute. How am I supposed to keep him a secret?

"Come on in." I step out of the entrance and point to the door leading to the basement. "You know the way down."

He groans. His shaky legs carry him inside. "Why do I always have to go down there? You got how many rooms in this monster house, a hundred, right? Why the basement? That place smells."

And he doesn't? "Basement or outside. And you'd better keep quiet or Mom will hear you. Now give me your keys so I can move your car before Dad gets home."

I park his car a block away, then hoof it back, arriving just as Dad's car pulls into the driveway. After dinner, I head to the basement. Uncle Leon is stretched out on the sofa. He has one arm over his face and doesn't move when I come down the stairs.

"Here." I hand him a plate of food. I sit on a box while he eats.

"Thanks. You're a good boy. And you're all I have."

"You have John," I say.

"No, I don't. That boy hates my guts. I really should have married Paula; I realized that too late. I got scared and didn't stop to think, and just ran. Now I have no one." He wipes his hand across his face. "At least John made something of himself. I am so proud of that boy."

"Tell him."

"What?"

"What you just said. You need to tell him."

He stares at the wall before shaking his head. "My boy doesn't need anything from a failure like me."

"What did you do, reject a real celebrity?" I ask.

"My old man and I went out and had a little too much the other night. I ended up with a shit-kicker hangover." He shakes his head. "I needed something to, you know, calm my head. They fired me over some policy about employee drinking. It was a club, for God's sake, what do they expect? Then my roommate kicked me out because I couldn't pay my half of the rent."

"Can he do that?" I ask.

"If Leon's name isn't on the lease, yes." Dad's voice comes from the top of the stairs. I knew he would find out. Just not this fast.

"There you go, trying to be a lawyer again," Leon says, looking up at him.

"There you go, being…" Dad stops and takes a deep breath. He doesn't even sound angry. Just tired and resigned.

Leon puts down the plate. "Go on, say it. You told me so. I'm just like our old man." Leon stands and grabs his shopping bag. He manages a weak smile. "At least I didn't hurt anybody."

Only my dad, I realize. *Only his whole family.*

After a minute, Leon struggles to his feet. "I know I can't stay. I won't cause any trouble, I'll go."

"And do what, sleep in your car?" Dad continues down the stairs, his tread slow and even. He looks at his brother and then at me. "Take Leon to the spare bedroom. Get blanket and pillows. And a pair of my pajamas."

"What about Mom?" I ask. "She'll have a fit."

"I'll take care of Celeste," Dad says.

"You always did," Leon says, as he follows me up the stairs.

Dad's hands curl into fists. "And you always wanted things you weren't willing to work for."

"What else are brothers for?"

I know Uncle Leon's words are meant to be a cut. Dad should tear into his brother. But my old man remains silent.

CHAPTER 33

The Farrington Flyer mascot—some poor dude forced to wear an orange-and-black bird suit—shakes T'Shawn's hand. I had promised I'd take T'Shawn to a basketball game. I promise myself I won't have to think. Not about Nicole, or my future son. Or daughter.

"Relax and enjoy the game," I say. I buy Coke and popcorn from a vendor. "We've got good seats, good eats, and you're about to watch one of the best teams ever."

Spencer drops into a seat down in front. He's still using a cane to get attention. A few people look from him to me and scowl, like I'm the bad guy. Don't they realize I'd have had to saw his leg off for him to still need a cane after all these weeks? Besides, he's too stupid to remember which leg is supposed to be hurt. Tonight, it's the right.

T'Shawn and I take seats near the top of the stands. Our location feels perfect, until I see Barney seated across the gym with some of her friends. She wears a denim jacket trimmed in black lace. Even from this distance, the big girl looks awesome. If the place wasn't so packed and the game about to begin, I would change seats and get closer to her.

And then what?

The cheerleaders begin their moves. Nicole isn't with them. I see her near the exit doors, talking with her sister. They must be having an argument, from the way Nicole is waving her hands. Does Giselle know about the baby? I think sisters probably share a lot. They continue arguing as the game starts. Julian takes the tip and we score first.

"Are we winning?" T'Shawn asks before taking a bite from his orange cotton candy.

Julian grabs a loose ball and passes to Cesare. Seconds later, a defender strips the ball from Cesare's hands. Chesterton scores. A chorus of boos fills the gym.

I stare down at the Chesterton forward wearing number twenty-four. He specializes in stealing the ball. He dribbles and feints; one of our guys stumbles and a whistle blows.

"Foul on number twenty-four," the ref says.

"You should be down there." T'Shawn slurps his pop and leans forward in his seat.

If I were, I'd be telling Nicole to stop doing all those jumps and flip-flops. That can't be safe.

Rumbles fill the stands as our team continues to sputter. Julian's the big guy in points, blocks, and rebounds. Cesare plays like a dipshit. Passes continue to slip through his hands. He makes a run for the basket and gets called for traveling. Chesterton players ignore him. They focus on Julian, double-teaming him whenever our team goes on offense, cutting him off so our guys can't get the ball to him. Chesterton moves ahead by ten points. The man Cesare should be guarding breaks free and scores. Boos fill the gym, all directed at Cesare. A whistle sounds. The boos turn to cheers when Kasili sends him to the bench. Cesare grabs a towel, throws it over his head, and sits with his elbows on his knees.

"That guy sucks," T'Shawn says.

The sound of bodies colliding forces my attention back to the court. Julian hits the floor and rolls around grabbing for his leg. Silence fills the gym as the trainer rushes out to examine him.

Julian gets up and shows the fans a sloppy grin as he waves at the crowd. He limps when he moves back into position, his grin twists and he seems to be in pain. The crowd groans like it's the end of the world. I see the fake. Julian went to a better acting school than Spencer. The other team ignores Julian until he suddenly accelerates and flashes past the guards to intercept a pass and score. The bleachers shake, people leap to their feet and scream approval and encouragement. I join in the yelling, even though I'm cheering for my biggest rival. Across the gym Barney laughs and jumps and throws her arms around someone. I stiffen until I realize it's only one of her girlfriends.

Just before halftime, I leave T'Shawn and head for the locker room. Cesare stops outside the door when he sees me. Sweat makes his hair stick to his forehead. He looks down, unable to meet my eyes.

"What's wrong with you?" I say, after the others are inside. "You played better than that in sixth grade."

"I'm doing the best I can."

"It's not your best. You look like you don't care and Chesterton knows it. They're ignoring you and double-teaming Jules."

"That's what Coach said."

"He's right." I hate agreeing with Kasili.

I hate losing Cesare.

"Why do you even care?" Cesare says in a voice so soft I barely hear it above the crowd and the half-time band. He pushes through the locker room door.

The cheerleaders form their pyramid without Nicole at the top. She's hanging on the sidelines, arguing with her sister again. Giselle wears the same sad and furious expression Cesare did. She has her arms wrapped around herself tightly, as if she struggles to keep herself from doing something she would regret afterwards.

I consider going over to talk to Nicole, but I don't need two rejections in the same day.

During the second half, Cesare comes alive and runs off six unanswered points, once again playing like he's part of the ball. With twenty seconds left, he makes a clutch three-point shot that brings us to within one point. But then Chesterton controls the ball as the final seconds tick down.

Cesare fouls the ball handler. It's the right move. The foul wasn't flagrant, just a tap, but it's Cesare's fifth, taking him out of the game. Kasili claps Cesare on the back while a chorus of boos erupt from people who don't understand that a good foul is a work of art. This one stopped the clock with four seconds left. That gives us a chance. The short guard who replaces Cesare is another sophomore. He hasn't seen much playing time and glances back at the coach as if hoping Kasili will change his mind and send someone else instead.

I hold my breath as the Chesterton player's first foul shot wobbles before falling through the net. The crowd groans.

T'Shawn crosses his fingers on both hands. "He'll miss the next one. I'm praying real, real, real hard."

"Three reals should do it." I don't dare pray. If the guy makes this shot, we're dead.

The ball bounces off the rim. Julian rises and seizes control of the ball, calling for a time-out as his feet hit the floor. Our team huddles briefly around Kasili. Everyone is there, including Cesare. I know Kasili is telling them to hang together and do the teamwork thing. I want to dive down from the stands and join them. I know what to do. Take the ball, push my way forward, and not let anything stop me. Earn a quick two and at least give us overtime and another chance to win.

The horn sounds. Julian takes the inbound pass. Good. He plunges for the basket just as I would. I know what he's going for. Only everyone in the gym knows what's coming too. Three players move to block his path to the basket. They have position. There's no way around them. If Julian tries to shoot, they will block the ball. If he tries to go through them, he'll earn a charging foul. The seconds tick down. There's no choice. He has to throw up the Hail Mary; it's the only chance.

I jump to my feet. "Shoot, Julian!"

Julian does what I wouldn't. He passes off to the little guard, the only Farrington player in position, left open by the players triple-teaming Julian. The guy pivots and takes a three-point jump shot before any Chesterton players can adjust. The ball falls cleanly through the net as the buzzer sounds.

I get sprayed with big drops of someone's leftover Coke as the victory celebration begins. T'Shawn screams so loud my ears hurt. Behind me, I see Barney rushing onto the court and grabbing Julian. They look good together, like they belong. Fire burns my guts, but there's nothing I can do. He's a good guy, the kind with no skeletons in his past and no baby-mommas in his future.

I have a duty to Nicole and my future child. I can't let myself feel anything for anyone else. Just watching Barney leaves me so horny it hurts. But the one I want, I can't have. And the one I can have…

I have to marry.

*

"No, you do not have to marry that girl."

"Don't do it."

"Be smart."

My cousin, granddad, and uncle all give me the same advice. My uncle added, "Abortion," as if I could handle another death on my conscious. Granddad said, "Have a drink," as if that would magically make everything disappear.

John says, "Talk to your dad." I sit on the sofa in his apartment. He straddles a chair.

"He doesn't need to know." Anyway, what would I say to him?

"He's going to know something's up when the baby wakes him up crying for a two a.m. feeding. Maybe sooner, like when you carry the new bride over the threshold."

"I hate you."

He laughs. "You need to see your face."

No, I don't, because I can see his. It's an adventure, I tell myself. A new life, a mountain to conquer, a new world to explore. I can do this. I'll say marry me; Nicole will be happy and say yes.

"Is this the girl you rescued from a gang attack?"

"It wasn't a gang, there was just one guy." I wish it were Barney. Then everything would be simple. "I'm talking about Nicole. Cheerleader, great shape, with a big red stripe in her hair."

"You change girls faster than a crack Nascar team changes tires." He sighs and shakes his head. "You'll be tired of this one before you say 'I do.'"

"I'll never get tired of my kid."

His brow furrows, as if something he sees on my face confuses him. "Which do you want most, the girl or the kid?" The silence grows. John tries again. "Are you looking for a soulmate or a new beginning? Are you in love with this girl?"

"I like Nicole." That will have to be enough.

"When is this baby due?" he asks.

"This summer, I guess."

"And when is the wedding?"

"No date yet." I shrug. "I haven't told Nicole we're getting married yet."

"You mean asked her?" John says in a dry voice.

"Yeah, sure, asked."

"'Cause girls like being asked."

I force myself to turn and stare into the mirror and search for the face of a father. John is right, I can't wait any longer. Nicole is avoiding school, avoiding me. That stops. I have to see Nicole. I need a drink.

I need the drink now.

Three steps take me to John's fridge. Inside, I spy the remains of a six-pack. My fingers wrap around a cold can and I flip the pop top.

John jumps from his chair and reaches my side faster than I've ever seen him move. "I don't think so. You need a clear head to figure things out. I've seen how fast you go from sixty to zero when you drink. This isn't the time to go sliding downhill. Marriage will change everything. Before you do anything else, have a paternity test done. Do it now, because if you find out you're not the father after you marry, it's too late."

"You sound like Uncle Leon."

"Don't insult me. And don't ever take advice on women or life from him. That man thinks he deserves a father-of-the-year award if he happens to remember my birthday. Which he doesn't, most years."

"Is that why you never call him 'Dad'? Does it bother you that he never married your mom?" I remember the hunger in Leon's eyes when he talked about John. Hunger, and pride.

John stares at his hands. He's quiet for so long, I almost forget my question. "No. Maybe. A little. I don't call him 'Dad' for the same reason he doesn't call me 'Son'. Leon Kaplan has never been a parent."

That's the reason I have no choice. I can't be a hit-and-run artist. For better or worse, I have a father. My kid deserves one too.

For once, I'll be like my Dad and take care of my mistake.

CHAPTER 34

How do I tell Dad?
Yo, new grandfather, wassup?
Yeah, that will work.

I step onto the porch late in the evening. Snow falls, glistening in the porch lights, covering the lawn and sidewalk. Not enough to have to shovel, just enough to make the world look clean. I can't be a father. This is a mistake. I can't imagine Nicole and me as parents.

Mom wrapped a scarf around my neck and pushed a cup of coffee in my hands before I walked out onto the porch.

Middle School gave us health class and the big warnings. Most guys laughed, but I remembered what happened to my parents. Because of that, I fought back the urge to score with a girl until my junior year, and when I finally did, I vowed to always use a condom. Every time my girl and I planned to get together, I had protection. Nothing should have happened, except...sometimes our get-togethers weren't exactly planned. I guess that is the definition of baby-daddy.

At least my brain still works. I can still do math. I know that nine months make a baby. Nicole could be three, almost four months along. That means this summer, maybe as early as June.

"Wanda had her twins." Dad's breath spurts out like tiny white clouds as he speaks. He lifts his cigar and adds, "Her husband came by handing these out. He's practically floating."

That's what Uncle Leon missed when he left Paula and John. Was Dad happy when he stayed and married Mom? Or just determined not to follow in his brother's footsteps?

"Will you two hurry up out there?" Mom calls from the doorway. "You'll catch your deaths of cold."

"Soon," Dad says, before leisurely blowing out a smoke ring.

"Men," Mom says in mock disgust before disappearing back inside the house.

I clear my throat and ask, "What happened when I was born?"

"You popped right out, hardly even cried. You were so easy, so quiet, Celeste was a little worried at first."

"What about Perry?"

"He was a first and they take their sweet time. There's nothing like a first."

Nothing like a first.

"Did you ever think about having an abortion instead of marrying Mom?" The words come out before I can think and once I say them, I can't pull them back.

"Is there something you want to tell me?" he asks

"I just wondered."

Dad removes the cigar from his mouth and coughs. "I dreamed of spending a lifetime with Celeste from the first moment I saw her. I was happy when I learned she was pregnant. It meant she would marry me. She wasn't sure about all the 'til death do us part' stuff. She was scared, but she had her child to think of." I can't see his mouth, but somehow I can feel him smile, as if he feels proud of what he did with a fifteen-year-old sophomore.

"Perry was your child, too."

He pauses. "Right. Our child."

Dad puts out the cigar and leans against the railing. "Something happens to me every time Celeste enters the room. Even if I don't see her, I always know when she's close. Back in the old days, when I was in school, they called it pheromones. Whatever it is, she still has it." He pauses and looks at me. "Or is that TMI?"

"No, I've just never felt that feeling." Not for Nicole. And it hits me. Barney is the one girl who makes me feel like I can relax and be myself. Because she knows what I am. Knows and likes me anyway. But she's only fourteen and the years separating us feel like forever. Not that it matters. Even if Barney is my right girl, I've found her too late.

"You're still young," Dad says.

"You were my age when you found Mom."

"And you're not me." Dad puts a hand on my arm and squeezes, and I feel closer to him than I ever have before. "Someday, you'll meet a girl who's different from all the others. For now just relax; there's no hurry. Life isn't a race."

Mine is. I have less than nine months.

*

I corner Nicole outside the gym after cheerleading practice. The girl I really want walks by with Julian. He mutters something in Spanish that makes Barney throw back her head and laugh. She smiles at the sophomore pretty-boy, revealing her mad awesome dimples. She puts a hand on his shoulder and her eyes shine as if he's the best thing she's seen all day, and the real reason she comes to school. I turn my back on them.

"I've been looking for you," I tell Nicole. "I've called, texted…why won't you answer?"

"Now you know what it feels like. Besides, we broke up, you thick-headed jock." She pushes past me as she speaks.

"Why didn't you tell me about the baby?"

She stops. Turns. Bites her lower lip. "How did you know?"

"Sometimes even thick-headed jocks can see the signs."

Players come out of the gym and walk past us; their practice is over too. Nicole glances around, her face tightening as if she feels trapped. Cesare comes out with the rest of the team.

"Who else knows?" Nicole asks in a hoarse whisper. "Did you tell Cesare?"

"Why would I say anything to him?"

"Thank God. This isn't easy for me, or my family." Nicole takes a deep breath and squeezes the papers in her hand until they rustle. "At least it will all be over soon."

"Over? What are you planning?"

"Everything is being taken care of. After this weekend there won't be a baby."

Abortion? "You can't do that."

"It's none of your business; you have nothing to say about anything."

I'm the father. I clench my fists.

"Why are you talking to him?" Giselle says from behind me. She glances from her sister to me.

"He's trying to interfere in our family affairs," Nicole says. She wants to keep things so quiet, I don't know if she's told Giselle the truth.

"You can't do this, I won't let you." I grab Nicole's arm.

"Do what?" Giselle asks.

"He knows," Nicole says. "He knows about the baby."

Giselle's face goes ashen.

"Get lost, Malik," Nicole says. "There is nothing more you can do. Stop trying to interfere."

"I'll call," I say.

"When?" Nicole speaks absently, as if my answer doesn't matter.

As soon as I figure out what to do.

Nicole puts an arm around her sister and leaves me.

CHAPTER 35

What am I going to do about…" I look around at the crowd, lean closer to Zach, and lower my voice. "About the baby."

Zach and I sit in the Coffee Hut, a place he calls his favorite caffeine distributor, located on the first floor of the building holding his law office. He's Mr. Peterson again, wearing the tie and dark brown suit that seems like the uniform of the guys who work here. These men and women rush around with suits and briefcases, and the attitude that they can do anything. Zach and I share a small table by the window. I can almost believe I imagined the chains and eagle tattoo. I don't have to imagine the lime. I smell that on his breath over the aroma of caffeine. I hope a heavy jolt will help clear my head. The sounds of machinery and muted conversation swirl around us.

I went to temple and mass over the weekend. Both had hard pews. Neither place brought answers. My cup doesn't runneth over. It's sprung a leak and will never be filled.

"What about father's rights?" I ask Zach. "It's my kid, I'm the father."

"She's carrying the child, so everything about the pregnancy, including any decision to end it, is up to her."

"That's why I called you. Get an injunction or something."

"If she wants an abortion, you can't stop her." When I growl, he adds, "That's the problem these days. People think a lawyer is also a magician."

"Are you saying you can't do anything?"

"I'm saying yes, I can take your money. No, I can't force her to have the baby. And don't expect me to keep you out of jail if you try to kidnap her and hold her captive until after the child is born." He puts down his coffee, steeples his hands and stares into my eyes. "Look, I understand you're feeling overwhelmed."

"I'm feeling fine," I say through gritted teeth.

"That doesn't reassure me. With people like me, fine has its own special meaning: fucked-up, insecure, neurotic and…"

"I don't get emotional." I remember the sign in Kasili's office used the word "fearful." Zach went directly to the point. "Is that lawyer humor?"

"No, I learned that from AA. My friends there explained that I couldn't be helped while I was fine, that first I had to come to believe."

"Believe what?"

"In something I have a feeling you don't trust, a power greater than yourself. Sometimes a man has to accept that he is powerless. He has to believe he cannot do everything and be ready to trust that something else can help."

"That's why I came to you. You expect me to trust you, right?"

"Only in court. Right now, I'm talking about a higher power, whatever that means to you. The hardest part is step one. Learning to look in the mirror and accepting that what we see isn't God, or a superman; that we're not all powerful, not even close. AA taught me to avoid taking the first drink."

"What's the big deal about the first drink?"

"That's the one that causes all the problems. Not the second, or the tenth, or the hundredth."

That can't be right.

"I'm not one of you. I passed the test at Ageless and left that drink on the table."

"And I applaud you."

"So you have to agree I'm fine." I expected him to argue. Part of me thought he had only pretended to leave, and stayed to spy on me and saw how much I drank once I ditched him and his friends.

"You don't want me agreeing that you're fine," he says with a wry smile. He stares off into the distance, his face tight and thoughtful. I don't know what he's seeing, but I bet it isn't the street outside the window. I wonder who my higher power would be, anyway? I'm Catholic and Jewish, but no God wants to hear from me. And I don't look into mirrors anymore.

After a few seconds he shakes his head. "There I go, preaching again. Sorry. Chavez gets after me about that evangelist thing all the time. I like helping people. Maybe that's one reason why I became a lawyer. I know that AA saved my life, just like Alateen saved my kids."

"What is Alateen, anyway?"

"A group for kids with parents like me." Zach's voice is heavy and sad. "My ex takes them to the meetings. I lived with my kids long enough to hurt them. My wife goes to Alanon for the same reason. We 'alkies' have a saying: anyone can get into AA, but you have to know someone to get into Alanon, or Alateen."

I know someone. My uncle, my granddad. My father knows them, too. He also knows me.

"Why does everything need a group?" I ask. "Can't one person help?"

"Some problems need more than one person, like my disease. Maybe something like Alateen could have made a difference for me when I was young. Maybe they could have convinced me my mother's drinking wasn't my fault. And your father, he could have used them, too."

"What's wrong with my dad?"

"Open your eyes." Zach taut voice makes me wonder if he wants to tell me to drop and give him twenty, or give me a swift kick. "Sometimes your father reminds me of my ex. Living with me left her feeling inadequate."

"Did you hurt her?"

"In the worst way possible—I promised I'd change and got her to believe me again and again, until she wound up doubting herself."

"Why would my dad doubt himself?"

"Take a look at yourself. Other people do, and they ask, if that man can't keep his own house in order, what can he do for others?"

"What I do has nothing to do with my father."

"What you do has everything to do with him. Like it or not, you are part of his house." He drinks his coffee, grimacing just as he did with his seltzer at Ageless. "Like I said, he's just like my ex. Poor woman worked herself crazy trying to keep things normal—on the outside, anyway. On the inside, we were both falling apart, until she admitted the truth."

"That she didn't love you?"

"That love didn't matter. It wasn't enough."

I jump from my seat and thrust my hands deep in my pockets. If my father has problems, it's not because of me. "I don't need this. All I care about is what I can do about the baby. If you can't help me with that, I might as well leave."

"There's you trying that geographic cure again." Zach sounds sad, but resigned. "Running from problems doesn't work if the problems go with you."

"I'm not running. I just…I need to do something."

"As long as you don't kidnap her, okay? My suggestion, go see her, see if the two of you can negotiate something," Zach says. "Show her you'll be there for her and the kid."

"I won't abandon her. She can't get rid of my kid, not if I'm willing to pay for my mistake."

"Suggestion number two, act like a man, and never let the girl think you consider the baby a mistake."

*

Giselle opens the door to the Mitchells' apartment. The place is filled with furniture and stuff bought with her mother's employee discount. I'm not complaining. The sofa is comfortable, even for a guy my size.

"What are you doing here?" Giselle says. "Where's Cesare? Did he send you? You can't change my mind." She cranes her neck, trying to look around me into the hall, as if she expects to see him on the stairs.

"Relax, I'm just here to see Nicole." I wait in the middle of the living room, uncertain whether to sit or stand.

"Nikki went to the store. She's mad at you."

"I know." I drop down on the sofa. I took every penny I'd saved to buy back my car and bought a ton of things for the baby. Acting like a man. I have to prove I can be responsible. I saved a little and bought the ring I pull from my pocket. It's sort of a friendship ring, but I figure, cheap as it is, it can still double as an engagement ring. "I'm here to give this to Nicole. I'm willing to marry her."

"You're *willing* to marry my sister?" She makes it sound like I said I was willing to strangle Nikki. "I thought you two broke up."

"You and your sister tell each other everything, don't you?"

"Mostly."

"Did she tell you she's pregnant? That I'm the father?"

"No. You're not." Giselle jumps like a model rocket exploding off the launch pad. I don't know why she's so surprised.

"I know what you're thinking. Yes, I'm sorry, yes, I'm a lowdown dog. I know your mother will want to kill me, but I'm here to fix things." There, I even remembered not to call it a mistake.

"Nicole isn't pregnant." She swallows. "I am."

Giselle's voice is so soft I need a few seconds to realize what I heard. Staring into her face, I realize she's telling the truth. Not me. Cesare. He's going to do the daddy thing.

I tell myself this is a good thing. I dodged a major league cannon-ball.

"Does Cesare know?" I ask.

"I can't tell him." A tear falls down her cheek. "He can't know about this, not ever."

"Relax, you own that guy. Maybe he'll be a little upset at first." Maybe a lot upset. But if I could stand up, he'll come through. Sometimes he acts much older than me. "Cesare thinks he loves you, so you'll be fine. He deserves to know he's going to be a father."

"What could I tell him? 'Remember that little argument we had a few months ago? I got mad and went out and did something unbeliev-ably stupid and, well, surprise! It's not yours.'"

*

Now that I know the truth, I see the signs.

I stand by my locker during passing period and watch the drama. Giselle avoids Cesare. She doesn't speak or turn her head when they pass in the hall. He stares after her, like an unwanted puppy that's just been shoved out of a car and is watching its masters drive off. Face pale, lips tight, he watches until she vanishes inside her classroom. Then he sighs and continues walking to the end of the hall. He almost bumps into Spencer and his cane.

I should have known Spencer was the kind of rat you always have to watch because he's willing to stab you in the back and smile doing it. Does he even know Giselle is carrying his kid?

CHAPTER 36

To join or not to join? Sooner or later, I will have to give Lamont an answer.

I want to ask John about the guy, without telling him about the offer. If I did, he'd probably just rip my side open again, take back his superglue, and go home. He claims the act of cutting ties with the gang raised his IQ by twenty points. He also swore he'd break both his half-brother's arms if the kid ever joined up.

"Leon wasn't happy with me until I joined the Enforcers; that's what it took to make him proud." He sighs. "Wasn't worth it."

"What about Lamont? What do you know about him?"

"Lamont's got brains, which makes him dangerous. The pushy little bastard wants to ratchet things up again. Unfortunately, he's got some folks listening to him. He hangs around the pool hall, taking people's money and plotting world domination. He's also got big plans and a bigger mouth. A lot of the old guard like him, but he's got enemies, too."

John wears his dark blue hospital's smock with long sleeves and two big pockets. Today's *kipah* is green, red, and black; it was crocheted by a former girlfriend. He has a steady J O B, so he easily attracts girls, until they find out how little his job pays. He pokes my wound with his finger. The glue has dissolved. My side is a little tender, a little ugly, but he looks pleased.

"There's no sign of infection," he says.

"You're good," I say. "You should go to med school."

"That's what my last date said. Have you any idea how many years getting an M.D. takes out of your life? Besides, nurses are the ones who really take care of people. I mean, doctors come in, prescribe a med or two, and disappear. And they never forget to bill you." He stares through me, eyes wide, like he's watching an impossible dream. "It's the nurses who do the day-to-day work that gets patients well."

"So, you don't want to be a doctor. I get that," I say. "But why not upgrade and become a registered nurse?"

He sits on my bed and begins wrapping and putting away his supplies. He moves slowly and more deliberately than necessary. "I've thought about going to college and getting a bachelor of nursing degree. That opens up doors, lets me do a whole lot more to help people. But even that takes time and money, or did you forget that?"

I guess I did.

"Ask my dad to help," I say.

"Ask me to help with what?" Dad stands at my door.

"I don't take charity," John whispers before flopping on the bed beside me and putting an arm around my shoulders. "Malik and I are ready to become a couple; we want your blessing."

Dad steps inside my room, his eyes fixed on me. "What happened to you, Malik?"

"It's nothing." I pull my shirt down.

"Your son is General Badass," John says. This time his voice is solemn. "He's a hero."

Dad looks from him to me. "What's John talking about?"

I poke my cousin in the back, trying to tell him to go silent.

John ignores me. "Your boy played hero and rescued a girl from a gang attack like some one-man SWAT team."

"Not exactly a gang attack." I will kill my cousin. The SWAT team thing sounds good, but it's not enough to save his life. I will kill him slowly and painfully, and leave tire tracks across his big mouth. Then I will kill myself for ever telling him anything.

"What happened? What girl?" My dad doesn't blink. I wonder if his expression holds disbelief or anger. When I say nothing, he turns back to John. "Did you help Malik with this?"

"I wasn't there; it's all on General Badass." John almost hits his head when he clicks his heels and pretends to salute me.

"It was no big deal," I say.

Dad clears his throat. "When were you going to tell me?"

Never. I shrug.

"Were you hurt?" His hand trembles as he removes his glasses and wipes his forehead.

"You mean did I hurt anyone? Don't worry, the cops won't come to the door with handcuffs to pick me up or anything. You don't have to worry about a scene."

A muscle jerks in his jaw. "I mean were *you* hurt?"

"Would it make a difference?"

"You're my son; of course it would." He replaces his glasses and takes a deep breath. "I wish you'd told me this before. Am I such a monster you can't talk to me?" His voice shakes, but it holds the soft, soothing tone I remember from my childhood.

"You're no monster." I realize we are alone in the room. I don't know when John left, but I'm glad it's just my dad and me.

We don't speak again. This is not our usual heavy silence. Tonight, I don't feel alone.

Dad pats my back. I realize I've done the impossible: I've made him proud.

I'm not letting that go.

CHAPTER 37

Lamont looks older, tired. Living in abandoned buildings must be hard. The lines in his forehead are as deep as the ruts left by trucks in dirty snow.

T'Shawn runs to greet his brother.

"You having fun, T?" Lamont grins and lifts his hand for a high-five. T'Shawn jumps, but Lamont raises his hand at the last second so the kid misses his. T'shawn groans.

"Is this heap of trouble getting to you?" Lamont asks me.

"T'Shawn's no trouble," I say.

"Yeah, I'm good with Malik." T'Shawn nods rapidly. "He took me to see a game and it was the bomb. Malik says he'll teach me how to dunk."

Lamont squeezes his brother's arm. "You need muscles first."

"Yeah, I know, but Malik says they'll come. He says I'm a natural. Malik is like my bestest friend ever."

"You talk a lot, Leaky-leaky." Lamont asks, cutting off T'Shawn's flow of words. He glances from the kid to me, like Sherlock seeking clues to a mystery. "I've been expecting to see you, but you never came back. I need to know where you stand: in, or out?"

"Out. I'll stay neutral." The answer is easy. I guess the gin is the only reason I ever considered his offer. I don't want his world.

"I don't believe in neutral. There are only two kinds of people in the world: prey and predator. People are either with me or…"

"Then I guess we both know where we are," I say. I'm on Lamont's shit list now.

I take T'Shawn's hand. "Let's go; I promised to get you home on time."

"That shelter isn't his home." Lamont's grip tightens on T'Shawn's shoulder.

"Hey," T'Shawn says and squirms.

"It's not a tug of war." I let go of T'Shawn.

Lamont grins and releases his grip on his brother. "Yeah, you better get going, T. Don't want to upset Moms." He begins walking away. The other guys follow him.

Everyone except Darnell.

"Too bad, Neuter," Darnell says, and smiles. "Sorry, I meant neutral."

He's not one bit sorry.

Lamont turns. "Let's go, Darnell."

Darnell takes a deep breath and shuffles into place with the others.

There's a power struggle going on, and Darnell and Lamont are in the thick of things. Lamont pulled someone down to get his spot. Darnell's one of dozens reaching to yank him aside. He looks ready to yank me down, too. But he's not Perry, and I'm not afraid.

CHAPTER 38

I pat my chest. "Check me out, Barney. I haven't had a drink in ages and it's all because of you." *Congratulate me.*

"Good," Barney says.

Just good?

It was hard, but I haven't been drinking. Except back when I was considering Lamont's offer, and I had to drink with him to keep him from considering me an enemy. And Granddad because he really hates drinking alone. But otherwise, I've been clean.

And I am not going to be a father.

Now that I'm free, I want another chance with Barney. I touch her arm. Shock waves run across my skin.

"Don't pretend you don't feel it too," I say.

"It's just chemistry." Barney's voice is high and breathless. "There's too much history between us."

"It's more than that. I want you to be my girlfriend. Forget the past and give me another chance. I've changed."

"I respect how hard you've worked to change."

"Respect isn't enough. What about forgiveness?" That's not what I want from her. Can't she see? Doesn't she feel?

"I forgave you a long time ago. But I can't let myself forget. That wouldn't be smart. That's what my mom did. He'd swear, she'd forgive him, then he'd hurt her again. I refuse, Malik. I won't fall into that trap." Her voice is calm. Too calm. "We're friends now. That's a good thing."

It's not enough. "I need you, Barney." That will do it. Girls can't help coming to the rescue when someone needs them. "I only changed because of you. Sometimes I feel like I'm holding onto a ledge by my fingertips. They're blistered and bleeding and you're the only thing holding me up. I'll drink again without you."

"Don't you dare try to put something like that on me," she says, her voice loud and angry. "I'm not responsible for what you do. Even zoo animals only do things when they really want to. You have a mind of your own."

"So do you, but when the time comes, you'll still be jumping on that bus and heading off to prison to see your old man again."

"It's not the same thing."

"Then don't go. Tell your aunt you refuse to go back. It's what you really want; you know it, and so do I. Your diary said…"

Wrong!

The alarm fills my head too late. The words are already in the air. There's no way to pull them back.

She jerks like I punched her. "I wrote all kinds of things in my diary. *My* feelings, *my* dreams. You stole it and used my feelings to hurt me. Nothing in there meant anything to you. You didn't care about me."

I did. I do.

My mouth goes dry.

She bites her lip before saying, "When you used my words and threatened David unless I agreed…would you…would you have really made me do it with you?"

"It? What are you, ten?" Dumb, but I can't answer her. I don't dare. Acid burns a hole in my stomach. It's like I'm back in jail, watching handcuffs being strapped around my wrists. I thought Barney wanted me back then, that she was just pretending to have second thoughts when she pushed me away. What if I'd had her alone and she had told me no? Would I have listened? I used to beg Perry to stop hitting me. I hated him for not listening.

How can I expect Barney to feel any differently about me?

I toss a glance up at the ceiling, hoping for something, anything. Silence. I look down. No quicksand around either. Just Barney, waiting for an answer.

"I need to know, Malik."

I suddenly realize, "You're still a virgin, aren't you?"

"Don't say it like it's a disease."

"I'm...surprised." Astonished. Shocked. Why didn't I realize?

"Would you have forced me to have sex with you?" she asks, her back stiff, her voice flat.

The acid burn grows, flaring from my stomach, up my throat, into my mouth. A lie hangs on my lips. *No, Barney girl, it was all a joke. I can't believe you thought I was serious. What kind of a-hole would try something like that?*

The kind who can't face himself in the mirror.

I guess Barney reads the truth on my face.

"Yeah, seems I was a silly kid chasing Halloween candy, not realizing how sick it would make me," she says. Her chin quivers, but she doesn't cry. "The worst thing is, when I first saw you, before I knew what you were like, I did want to be your girlfriend. You seemed like everything heroes were supposed to be."

Ashes fill my gut as the girl who once respected me turns away. Her steps echo as she walks down the empty hall.

CHAPTER 39

Barney is already at the Outlet when I arrive. She throws right crosses at the face on the bag. She used a marker to scribble my name under that face.

"The girl's a natural," Ed says. "Or maybe she just hates you."

"Means I trained her right," I say.

And she hates me.

Barney stops punching when she realizes I'm standing next to her. I put my hands behind my back and say, "You get the first blow." I owe her this.

"What?" She takes a quick look around the gym and then puts her gloved hands against her waist.

"Hit me." I lift my chin to present her with a target.

"Don't mess with me."

"I'm not joking."

The guys gather close and yell encouragement to her.

"Hit him."

"Knock him out, Barney."

"Go on, girl."

Blam.

She goes for my stomach, not the jaw. I wasn't ready for that. I'm down on the floor. The girl has power. Guys all over the gym applaud and yell congratulations. Just my luck, someone pulls out a phone and snaps pics.

"Was that supposed to fix something?" She kneels beside me as I struggle to regain my breath.

"Yeah."

"Well, it didn't. I don't get my jollies hitting people. Not even a badass."

"Former badass." I never liked that word anyway.

She shakes her head and returns to working on the heavy bag. Ed throws me a you-stupid-schmuck grin.

I grab my jacket and leave. Zach would laugh and say it was another "geographic cure," but I can't stay without looking at her and seeing how totally she ignores me. I hear a commotion at the end of the hall, near one of the utility rooms. I see a small crowd, including Nicole, Giselle, and a near-rabid Cesare.

Giselle clutches at Cesare's arm. He pulls free and hurls his shoulder against a door, trying to break it in like they do on cop shows. The hinges groan as if begging for permission to surrender.

"You have to do something," Nicole says, as I come close. "Giselle listened to you. Instead of having the abortion, she told Cesare, and now he's out for blood."

People should never listen to me, not ever.

"It wasn't my fault, she wanted me." Spencer yells through the door.

"You're a dead man." Cesare kicks the wood.

I grab Cesare and pull him away.

Cesare squirms in my hold. "Let me go. You don't know what he did."

"I know. Giselle told me."

"Why didn't you tell me?"

"It wasn't my secret to share."

"I'll beat him bloody, I'll kill him."

"That just puts you back in jail and turns everything I gave up into nothing. It leaves Giselle with nothing. And your father."

He jerks, looking surprised to hear me mention his old man. I can't believe I'm the one being reasonable. But I understand fathers better than ever before.

"Malik, is that you?" Spencer looks through the small glass window set high in the door. "Call off your crazy dog."

"You bastard, you raped my sister," Nicole screams.

"No way," Spencer yells. "She never said no." He must be suicidal. A smart guy would pretend he was sorry, or at least stay quiet.

"She's pregnant," Cesare yells. "What are you going to do about that?"

"Why do I have to do anything? It was just one time, and then you two kissed and made up. You probably did the deed."

"Giselle and I never have," Cesare says in a strained voice. He stops fighting me. When I release him, he goes to a corner, slides down the wall, and puts his arms around his knees.

Giselle sobs with her head on Nicole's shoulder.

I step to the door and stare at Spencer's shaking chin. "You have one chance to get out of here whole. Take it."

A few seconds later, the lock clicks. Spencer opens the door cautiously. His face is sweaty, and his eyes roll in his head as he looks around. He steps out, accompanied by the smell of loosened bowels with him. I wonder how long he's been F.I.N.E.

"It's not my fault," he says. "She used me. I'm the one who had to listen to her go on and on about what a dork her boyfriend was, and how he deserved a lesson. We downed a few drinks, smoked a little weed, and enjoyed ourselves."

A few drinks, using a girl to hurt another guy. I could be listening to myself.

"Spencer's right," Giselle says in a soft voice. "After that stupid, useless argument, I did go out with him. We started talking and…and it happened."

Cesare stands and goes to her. She releases her sister and steps into his arms. He looks at her like there's no one else in the world.

"Is that why you agreed to our arrangement?" I ask Spencer.

He doesn't pretend to misunderstand me. "I didn't think you'd really go through with the deal. Then I didn't care."

"Even I barely remember what happened that night," Spencer says. "It's the meds. My parents took me to some doctors who prescribed stuff that's supposed to make things better, but the pills just leave me feeling loopy and useless."

"So you don't take them, and you use drugs instead?" Barney's voice comes from behind me. She steps up to my side. Her lips are tight, eyes narrowed.

"Marijuana works better then Depakote," Spencer says. "Even beer beats that crap."

"What's Depakote?" I ask. Some kind of street drug I've never heard of?

"Medicine. It's a mood stabilizer," Barney says. "After I tried to…" She glances at Spencer and her voice deepens. "After I tried to kill myself, the doctors talked about prescribing Depakote for me. In the end they decided I didn't need it."

"See?" Spencer smiles like she made his point for him. "Told you I don't need that crap; it turned me into a zombie."

"I said *I* didn't need medication." Barney looks from Spencer to Cesare to me. I see the pain in her eyes. Old pain caused by her father. New pain that's all because of me.

Spencer throws a nervous glance around. I see it now, the way gravity seems to pull him down harder than anyone else. Something in his body seems to cry out that the world isn't right; even his eyes are only half-open. He trudges down the hall. Cesare stares after him, but he keeps his arms around Giselle. Her face remains pressed into his shoulder.

"I heard what Spencer said about a deal," Barney says. "Cesare beat Spencer and you took the punishment to protect him, didn't you?"

"We protected each other. We always have."

"You should tell people the truth. They might stop hating you if you did."

"Do you hate me?" I ask the question that shouldn't matter, but somehow means everything.

"No, not hate. I won't waste any more energy on hate. Not on you, not even my father. You were right when you told me to move forward and stop seeing my father. I did what you said, told him and my aunt there'd be no more visits. He wasn't happy, but my aunt understood."

Barney touches her hair, and suddenly I feel like a fish caught by a lure. I can't stop looking at her. The sight of her curves flowing through her bulky sweater turns my body into one action-packed lesson for a seventh grade sex-ed class. There's just too much they never, ever told us way back then. I reach for her hands and touch the wristbands covering her scars.

She pulls free and walks away, and I know that nothing has changed. She still wants nothing to do with me.

CHAPTER 40

Nicole takes Giselle home. Cesare and I head to the gym for some one-on-one while we fight our own problems. I want my friend back.

I finger the scar on my side. Time heals nothing by itself. That's the mistake our fathers made. Healing takes work.

I pick up a ball. Without a word, we begin a one-on-one. We don't need words—it's enough that we're on a court together. He dribbles once and takes a shot. The ball sails over the rim. It hits the floor. The bounces echo louder than the roar of blood in my head.

I scoop up the rolling ball, drive for the basket, and send it swishing through the net. I pick up the ball and pass to Cesare.

He lets the ball go through his hands. "It feels like I let Spencer win."

"Be real. You made the guy shit his pants."

"'Spencer shits.'" Cesare throws back his head and laughs. "Bet that's been retweeted a few hundred times already."

He looks at me, and for a moment, the bond between us is as strong as ever. I grab onto that moment and work to make it last.

"Spencer is just a one-pump chump with a tiny ego," I say. "It must have killed him when she went back to you."

"Giselle wants an abortion. I told her not to." Cesare retrieves the ball and takes a shot.

"Why?"

"That's what she said. 'It's not yours, so why do you care?' But Giselle is mine, you know. She's my girl, so the baby is sort of mine, too. For right now, nothing changes. We'll just take one day at a time and see what happens." He rubs his eyes. "Growing up is hell."

"Tell me about it."

"What about you?" he asks. "Maybe Nicole will want you back."

"I hope not."

A smile ghosts across his face. "You and Barney, huh?"

"You know?"

"I saw how you looked at her."

"I want her to want me."

"You mean you're whipped." He nods as if he's won some bet.

I guess he has, because he's right.

"This still isn't fair to you," he says. "You're still taking the blame."

"I'm okay with things the way they are."

"What if I'm not? What if I need to be punished?"

I know how that feels. I know about the pain that grows until you have to explode and you don't care who hurts—you or the world or both. I also know my worst punishment was losing Cesare. That can't happen again.

"If I give you a punishment, you have to accept things; no matter what it is or how bad, you can't back down." I know how he feels. And I know how to end this.

"I'm not in grade school, Malik. I don't need a double-dare. I agree, no matter what." A resolute note fills his voice.

"Okay then. Your punishment is—you have to be my friend again. No respect required."

"That's not punishment." He runs a hand through his hair. "You're still paying the price. You have to go to that shelter every weekend."

"I like the place. I may never stop going." They need me. Connie gave me the front-door code so I can come whenever I want, like a regular member of the staff. She also handed me a list of things for me to do that stretches into the summer. To make sure T'Shawn and I get to stay together, I helped his mother get Wanda's job after she followed through on her threat to retire with the twins.

"You lost your car," Cesare said.

"But there's this awesome wreck in the shop. I won't need much to buy her from the insurance company; they think she's totaled. I can have her rolling like a queen in no time, especially if you help."

"But the team. You're off the team."

"You guys are winning without me. Besides, the season's coming to an end soon." Losing the team still hurts, but not so badly now. It's like the scab covering the wound in my side. The skin beneath isn't fully healed, but picking at it is kind of satisfying, even though it stings.

"I'll accept your punishment," Cesare says.

"There is one more thing."

"I knew it." He squares his shoulders like a weary soldier facing a firing squad. "Tell me what I have to do."

"There's this essay I'm supposed to write. The judge wants to see it like, yesterday, and I never got started. You have to finish it for me, like right now."

He laughs, and I join him before adding, "And from now on, play like you mean it. That way you can still be a Fighting Illini and we can be roommates, because I'ma be the best walk-on they've ever seen."

He blinks rapidly. "Fine, you got it. Russo and Kaplan."

"Kaplan and Russo; say it right."

CHAPTER 41

The school called earlier. Somehow T'Shawn walked out of the building during recess and never returned." Connie wipes a shaky hand across her face. "I should have let you know so you wouldn't make a trip out here for nothing."

T'Shawn's mother stands beside her, crying. "It's so cold out there. I hope he's with his brother."

"The police are searching." The lines in Connie's forehead are deeper than ever.

I start searching, too, heading for Lamont's old hangout. The building is now totally abandoned. A rat stares at me lazily, barely pausing from the job of licking the open end of a gin bottle. The vermin officially own this dump now, along with the trash the other gangbangers left behind. This is what my father wants to change.

Lamont likes pretending he's a pool shark, so I try the nearby pool hall that doubles as a bowling alley. The place used to be filled with families and bowling leagues in the evenings. Now it's nearly empty. Only two lanes are in use. There are four guys in the back playing pool. None of them belong to Lamont's crew. But I do find my granddad.

He looks like he's molded to a barstool, holding a near-empty beer mug and watching a Bulls' game on a wall-mounted TV. He yells at the bartender, cursing the man for moving too slow. He reaches into his pocket for money. His hand moves with an exaggerated slowness that shows he's already a few beers past drunk, and he curses when he spills coins and bills on the floor.

The owner of the place grabs my arm. "Get your grandfather out of here. He's driving away what few customers I still have."

"Have you seen Lamont?" I ask.

"No, thank God, he's been M.I.A. these last few days. He's another one costing me regular customers. Families stopped coming in after he and his crew made my place a hangout. And I've already had cops in twice today looking for him."

"Why not tell Lamont and his crew to stay out?"

He groans like a car stuck in neutral, as if the thought had never occurred to him. Then he scowls and shakes his head. "Have you seen that big guy running with him? No way. I don't mess with the gang."

This man is a coward. No wonder my dad won't leave; the neighborhood needs people like him and Frank. "If you give up, they win," I say. "Get a clue or learn to live with it."

"I don't know what to do. I'll be out of business if this keeps up."

"More for Dwayne to gobble up," Granddad says. He stands behind me, alcohol fumes oozing from his pores.

The owner gives me a look and mouths the words, "Get rid of him," before walking away.

"My favorite grandson," Granddad says, and lifts a fist to start the ritual.

"I'm not playing that game anymore." My shoulder thanks me when I step out of reach.

His smile vanishes. "What's wrong with you, boy?"

"I'm not a boy."

"Don't get testy, you know what I meant. I treat you like a man. I'm the only one who does."

"Well, this man isn't playing."

He stares at me for a long time, digesting my words.

"Let me get you home," I tell Granddad. "You've had enough."

"I say when I've had enough." Granddad moves his hand in a sweeping gesture, waving to the bartender. "Another beer. My grandson is thirsty."

The bartender looks at me as he pours another mug, and never asks for identification.

The drink tries to call to me again, like a siren promising me Wonderland. I know things will look better if I drink. I won't worry about T'Shawn or anyone except myself.

But I can't let that happen.

"I can't drink," I say. "I'm still on probation."

"No one's going to say anything." Granddad flicks a hand through the air like he's waving away a fly. "Stop worrying. You don't want to be a jellyfish like Dwayne, scared of his own shadow."

He still thinks my father is nothing.

He's wrong.

Every word he says about my dad proves how little he knows his own son. The Dwayne Kaplan he describes is not my father, it's an imaginary creature. My father had to grow up listening this man and his brother both disrespecting him. How did he do it? Who could listen to this day after day and ever believe in himself? Somehow, my father managed. He believes in himself. He believes in me.

Granddad doesn't know Dwayne Kaplan.

He doesn't know me.

I stare into a mirror on the wall behind the bar. I don't see the second coming of Perry Kaplan.

There's only me.

"You have to watch out for jellyfish," I say. "They only seem weak until you mess with them. Then they make you real sorry, real fast."

"What's that supposed to mean?" Granddad actually looks puzzled.

"It means no more one-for-the-road, no more drinking buddy." I almost laugh because I've never seen anything so clearly before. "I love you, but I'm not playing these stupid games with you anymore. If you don't want to leave, I can't make you. But I'm going. I need to find Lamont."

The deep lines on Granddad's face smooth into a smile. "Changed your mind, eh? I figured you would."

"What do you mean?"

"I asked him to take you on, and you blew it."

Why am I surprised?

"Do you know where he is?" I ask.

"Lamont is going places," Granddad continues. "You'd be wise to let him take you along."

"Just tell me where to find him," I say. "I'm eager to join up."

The lie gets him moving. I'm not surprised when he leads me to another abandoned building. The walls protect the interior from the wind, but a broken window means it's still crazy cold on the inside. Ice from a broken water pipe clings to a wall. Ragged laughter flows from more than one throat. Laughter, followed quickly by a muffled sob. The back of my neck itches from more than stray cobwebs. Life-In-The-Hood lessons one through ten flash through me, all saying, "Get the hell out of here."

Now!

But this is all about T'Shawn.

We enter a musty room. The sharp, savage odors of alcohol and stale urine are only a few of the sour smells in the air. Several figures stand inside.

"Hey, old man." Lamont steps forward. "And you brought Leaky-leaky with you."

"Malik's come around," Granddad says. "My boy's ready for a tombstone of his own."

"Not true," I say, hoping my eyes don't show my fear. I look around the room. "T'Shawn, you here, buddy?"

What I thought was a pile of old clothes in a corner moves. I see him, sitting on the floor with his knees drawn up under his chin.

"Hey, guy." I walk over to crouch at his side. "People are looking all over for you. Your mom's worried sick."

"La-Lamont said it was time to blow." His teeth chatter.

"Well I'm blowing you back home." I take off my jacket and wrap it around him, pretending I don't see the moisture on his face. Then I grab his hand. He stands and we begin walking to the door.

Lamont steps in front of us. "My brother stays with me. It's time for him to be a man."

"I'm not leaving without him," I say.

"Do you think you can stop me and my guys?" He waves at the men scattered around the room.

There are six of them, including Darnell. No one's got my back; Granddad will be no help at all. Darnell cracks his knuckles and grins. The room is small. In a fight, T'Shawn could be hurt. But I can't go without him. All I'll be able to do is get in the first blow. Lamont has no reason to worry.

Lamont.

He doesn't know how to do the brother thing any better than Perry did. But he cares about T'Shawn.

I uncurl my fists. I can work with that.

"You said you wanted to be like my brother." I wait until Lamont nods before adding, "Maybe he was a great Enforcer, but he was one lousy brother."

"Don't be saying bad things about Perry," Granddad says. "He was a…"

"A hero on the streets, I know." You can never say anything bad about a dead hero. That's why no one tells the real truth about the way he died. "Want to know what really killed him?" I ask Lamont.

Granddad jumps in front of me and starts up the speech he made at the funeral. "Everybody knows he was poisoned, put down by a rival too gutless to face him man-to-man. The police wouldn't even investigate, they didn't care, what's another dead banger?"

"You know exactly what happened," I say.

"You're talking crazy." Granddad talks so fast that spit sprays from his lips. "You were only twelve, you don't know."

"I was there." I've revisited that scene over and over again in nightmares. The great and powerful gang hero dragged his little brother off to a party with his posse. I was always Perry's personal little show-and-tell. Well, tonight it's my turn to tell what happened. "Perry did it to himself

Mom was in the hospital having another operation on her hand. Dad was with her. Perry yanked me along with him. It wasn't so bad at first. He forgot about me and I hung with the older boys, listened to music, talked and drank beer. And when someone said "trail mix," I thought they meant the real thing. Until I saw the contents of the bowl they handed me.

They all laughed when I said no.

"Are you sure the little coward is related to you?" one said.

"I think someone made a mistake." Perry pushed me away and grabbed the pills I had refused. "More for me," he said and swallowed.

He was dead before dawn.

"After years of hurting me, Perry got stinking drunk and downed God only knows what drugs, because he wanted to. The worst thing is, I couldn't even feel sorry. I remember the emergency room and the funeral and…and I don't remember ever once being sad that he was gone. Is that what you want to be, the guy T'Shawn doesn't even mourn?"

"I won't hurt my brother," Lamont says. T'Shawn keeps my jacket huddled around his head.

"You're hurting him now," I say.

"T wants to be with me."

T'Shawn looks up. "No, I don't."

I walk over to him. "What do you want?"

"I want Mama." There's no hesitation in his voice.

"Who takes a ten-year-old he cares about away from his mother to live like this?" I ask Lamont.

He puts his hands on his head and kicks the wall.

"T'Shawn and I are leaving now." I take the boy's hand.

Lamont continues blocking the door.

T'Shawn sucks in a deep breath and wipes his face, leaving moist streaks under his eyes. "Please, Lamont. I want to go home."

"Shut up, you little coward," Darnell says.

Lamont releases his fury by punching Darnell. "You don't get to give orders around here. I'm still in charge."

There is no respect in the look Darnell throws Lamont. The silence feels like pressure. This isn't over, and I don't see how Lamont ever turns his back on the guy. Or why the older guy obeys Lamont.

Lamont looks at me, and his brother. "Take T. I need to be able to move fast anyway. He'd just get in the way."

I did it. No knife, no blood. It feels too easy, but I've won.

CHAPTER 42

The text reads, *Malik Anderson Kaplan, get home NOW!*

I don't need to see a 911, and I don't need to check who the sender is. I rush home. Mom stands in the living room with both hands thrust into her waist, a position her scars make painful. She's surrounded by boxes and they all have the logo of the baby store. I forgot to cancel my order.

"You want to tell me what all this means?" she asks.

Not really. "Nothing, Mom."

"If I'm going to be a grandmother, that is something."

"You're not. There is no kid, okay? I made a mistake." I begin gathering boxes. "I'll get this junk back to the store."

"You thought there was a child. You were getting ready to welcome it." Mom pulls me around and places her hands on my shoulders. "I am so proud of you."

I wrap my arms around her and pull her tight, inhaling her perfume.

She squirms a little and then laughs. "What are you doing?"

"Don't tell me you forgot the bear hug special." I growl.

"I never forgot. But sometimes I wondered if you did. We used to be close, until my accident." She touches the ridged flesh on the side of her neck. "I was afraid the scars bothered you."

"Not the scars, Mom. I just wished I could have fixed things for you."

"You were only a little boy; it wasn't your job to fix anything." She pulls free and looks around the room. "For a guy, you're doing pretty good. Your father never thought about half this stuff."

"Why did you marry him?" I snap my lips shut, too late to contain the question I already know the answer to. She never had a choice.

Mom jerks and her eyes close so tightly it seems like she's trying to shut out a nightmare. "I knew one of my sons would ask someday. All these years and I still have no answer ready for you."

"It's okay, I shouldn't have said anything."

"No, it's time I told someone. Your father was the geek who stared at me as if I wasn't real. He loved me, so he agreed to marry me, even though it meant accepting another man's son as his own."

We head for the kitchen, where I fix coffee. She nods gratefully as I hand her a cup.

"Dwayne was one of the good guys. Quiet, head stuck in a book…except when I caught him staring at me." She sips her coffee and sighs. "Like a lot of girls in school, I couldn't stay away from Leon. He was the kind of super bad guy that just sucked us in. I don't excuse myself. Deer may get mesmerized by bright lights, but I'm a human being. I wasn't Leon's only trophy, just the one foolish enough to let herself get pregnant."

"He wouldn't marry you?" I lift my cup to my lips the minute I say those stupid words. She's talking about my I'm-loose-meat-and-will-never-be-caught Uncle Leon.

"When Paula Henley became pregnant with John, Leon used her as his excuse for not marrying me. I was his excuse with her. Convenient to have two baby-mommas at the same time."

"I once had three girlfriends at the same time," I say, and then bite the inside of my mouth. Some things should never be said in front of Mom.

"Are you proud of that?" She lifts a hand before I can find an answer. "Don't tell me, I don't really want to know that much about my teenaged son's love life. Leon told me the baby was my problem, not his. I felt broken." Mom's words grow toneless. "I kept the pregnancy hidden until morning sickness hit and my parents insisted on taking me to a doctor," she says. "Dwayne came and asked me to marry him."

"Did he know Leon was Perry's father?"

"Leon told him. He boasted. Dwayne said he didn't care, that he'd loved me for a long time. Before then, I had barely noticed him, that's how stupid I was. When I finally took a look, I saw a good guy. He had a future, a scholarship to the University of Wisconsin. He was getting out and going places. Taking on a wife and child killed his dreams."

Mom brushes sweat from her cheek. At least I think that's sweat. "My family was happy to accuse Dwayne of every sin in the world." She gave a nervous little laugh. "He accepted every rotten thing they said until I hurt so much for him, it became love. I realized that I had married the right Kaplan brother after all. As for my family, if not for my children, I wouldn't have anything to do with those sanctimonious assholes—oh, God." Her scarred hand goes to her lips.

"I'm old enough, Mom, you can say the word."

She drops her hand and laughs. "You're a man, just like Dwayne was. Like he is. He struggled for years to take care of Perry and me."

"And then I came along and made things worse."

"Oh no, you made us complete. You were the baby Dwayne wanted, from the moment you were conceived."

Perry used to like calling me names. Fat boy. Douchebag. Coward. Mostly I didn't believe him. Except the fat boy thing. Maybe even douchebag. And the coward part. I guess I really did believe what he called me. All except his favorite claim:

You're not my real brother.

Did Perry know? And what about Dad? Dwayne Kaplan, the chump who took the blame and married a girl because the real baby-daddy, his own brother, wouldn't. I know from Biology class, there are animal species where the male kills his mate's young if he isn't the father. Lions, bears, apes, even dolphins. They can tell just by the way the kid smells. And then there are the ones who raise the cuckoo child, kids that don't even resemble them, but they feel the call of duty and fill the demanding stranger's mouth.

Duty.

That's the kind of man Dad is.

Mom picks up a box and turns it around in her hands. "I almost wish I were about to be a grandmother. You even remembered to buy a bottle warmer. You got all the cozy things that didn't exist when you were a baby. It would be a shame to just send all this back to the store."

"I think I know someone who might need this stuff," I say.

"Then we'll gather it all together and make a delivery."

"I'll handle things."

"No." She rubs her hands together. "It's time I got out of the house and back into life. And it's good to know my shopping gene was passed on—that, and Dwayne's chivalry. Now get moving, we have a lot to do."

CHAPTER 43

I find Dad in the basement, standing beside the ratty sofa. I remember why this sofa means so much. How could I have let myself forget? Barney's not the only one who tried to kill herself.

After Mom survived the explosion and fire, after three weeks in the burn unit, and coming home to an agony no painkiller could touch, she decided to die. I saw her sitting on this sofa, holding a butcher knife. I heard Dad beg her to put the knife down and stay with him. He placed a hand on her shoulder and bent his head over hers like a giant Atlas, and begged. I always considered him solid, unbending, someone who might crack or break, but never yield. I had never thought about all the weights he carried before. He didn't bend or break. Not until she put down the knife. Then he knelt and cried.

Dad looks colossal standing there now, an Atlas once again. I never realized there could be so much strength in quiet. I get why the alderman listens to him, why the mayor wants him. I'm glad he changed his mind and agreed to join the task force.

He glances at me and then looks away. But before he turns his head away, I see the haunted look in his eyes. He doesn't know how to start. But I do.

I take a deep breath, determined to get this right. The faint odor of cigar smoke helps me relax.

"Do you know why I played basketball?" I ask.

"Because you're a great ballplayer."

The words of praise sound awesome. But they aren't the only truth. "Because Perry played football. I had to do something else, anything else. I needed to be different, but it didn't work. I'm too much like Perry. I drink. I drink a lot. Then I do things I hate. Things I wish I could forget. So I drink more, only that makes things worse." I push the words out in a rush before I have time to change my mind about confessing.

Something flashes across his face, an emotion I can't read. For a moment, I wonder if I've disappointed him again. Then the man who really treats me like an adult comes close and puts his arms around me. I'm too big for him to hug, too old, but I let him because I want to feel close.

When he steps back, he asks, "What do you intend to do about this, son?"

"I don't want to drink anymore."

"Have you had a drink today?"

"I won't drink today. But I don't know what I'll do tomorrow." I sit down on the sofa and stare at my hands. Tomorrow. Next week, next year—how do I know?

"Today is what counts," Dad says. "One day at a time; it's the only real way to stay sober. Remember that every time tomorrow becomes today."

"I can't do this alone."

"I promise you won't have to." He shakes his head wearily. "Insanity of the mind doesn't begin to cover the way I was. Am, still, really. I always believed that somehow I made my father drink because I wasn't a better son. I grew up making excuses for him and doing his work because God forbid the poor man suffer the consequences of his actions. You'd think with my history, I'd have seen what was happening inside my house to my own son." He sighs heavily. "For a long time I wasn't sure I knew how to be a real son. Maybe that's why I never learned how to be a real father."

"You are a real father." I can't believe I once thought life would be easier without him.

"When I saw the signs in Perry, I jumped to the rescue again. I tried to force him to straighten up. Everything I did made him worse. I made a one-eighty with you, hoping the hands-off approach would work better. Apparently, you ended up thinking I don't care."

"I know about Perry," I say. "About Mom and Uncle Leon."

"Don't blame her." A protective growl rumbles from his throat. "Perry hated having me around. I understood. I spent my childhood praying my father would stay out of my life. I couldn't be a part of anything because I knew he'd eventually show up and leave me embarrassed. I vowed I'd never embarrass any child of mine that way, so I stepped back, from his life, and from yours."

"You don't embarrass me. I'm not Perry."

"Then you're stuck with me." The cushion sags when he sits down beside me.

"I have a feeling I'll be sorry about this someday," I say. Dad's quiet gaze tells me he knows what I really mean. More time with him will keep me away from temptation, a good thing since I'm not Zach.

"You talk about not being Santa Claus and people learning from mistakes, but you still take care of them. Don't pretend you don't pay Granddad's rent. The shelter—Connie said she'd have had to close. And the community center. You're Anonymous, aren't you?"

His breath hitches. "The neighborhood really needs someplace for kids to go; that's all. This is my place, my 'hood,' I was born here and I believe staying here is the right thing to do." The force of his voice shocks me. His lips are tight, eyes hooded like thunderclouds, and I see why even the mayor listens to him.

"Take back the streets," I mutter.

"The streets never went anywhere. And neither will I. I won't run or let my neighborhood go down a toilet. I believe I can change things. Too many people take all they can and then leave. I show people becoming something more is possible, that I don't have to tear someone else apart to own 'turf.'"

"But respect, don't you want that?"

"No one takes away my self-respect, and that's the only kind that really counts. Unless you mean fear. I don't need anyone afraid of me. Least of all my son. The first time I saw you, you were so tiny and perfect. I couldn't believe I'd had a part in making you. My damned God complex. I told myself if you grew up to be anything less than perfect, it would be because I screwed up."

"You gave yourself too much credit."

We sit silently for a moment. Then he grins.

"Your mother and I made some special memories here." He pats a sofa cushion. "This is the spot."

He can't mean… "No, Dad, don't say it."

"You were conceived right here. This poor couch saw many workouts."

"TMI, Dad." I jump to my feet. I'll never sit there again.

CHAPTER 44

Zach offers to be my Alcoholics Anonymous sponsor.

"I guess I've come to believe," I tell him.

"You guess?" He sounds fierce, like I'm the opposing prosecutor and he has some tricky point of law to prove that beyond a reasonable doubt thing.

"Okay, I believe."

"Then the easy stuff is done; get ready to do real work." He rubs his hands together like some comedy villain. "I'm gonna enjoy making you sweat."

The first three steps of Alcoholics Anonymous will be really hard.

1. We admitted we were powerless over alcohol—that our lives had become unmanageable.

2. Came to believe that a Power greater than ourselves could restore us to sanity.

3. Made a decision to turn our will and our lives over to the care of God *as we understood Him.*

The ninth step, making amends to the people I've hurt, will actually be the easiest. I've already begun with Cesare, Giselle, and my Dad. Zach told me to slow down, but I'm an over-achiever. And I really want to reach out to Barney. She has to work until closing tonight because another waitress called in sick, so I wait until late before heading to Frank's place. I don't expect the free coffee, I don't think she will even want me around. But I gave myself the job of watching over her. No matter what she thinks about me, I'll keep doing that.

The wind blows scraps of newspaper down the street. The Blue line train rumbles overhead. The sign on the door reads "Closed," and the lights are off inside Frank's place. I grab my phone and check the time. Five minutes before closing. The last time Frank locked up early was the day his mother died. I lean close and peer through the window. A sliver of light shines from under the kitchen door.

I try the front door. The knob turns.

This is totally wrong. I pull out my phone and start to dial.

"Nope," a voice says from behind me. Something smashes into my back. My phone drops into the snow. I turn to see one of Lamont's crew, a wide-eyed, jerky kid. I send a right jab to his nose. He groans and takes a step back. His breath comes in hallow gasps. I grab him by the collar. By the time I see the knife, I'm too close to avoid the blow that pierces my shoulder.

He shoves me, forcing me inside the restaurant.

"Look what I found," he calls out. He pushes me into the kitchen. I stumble inside, blinking in the sudden light. Grease and the smell of hot java from the pot still sitting in the coffee maker fill the room. Lamont, Darnell, and another guy stand around the room. Add in the guy pushing me and the odds totally suck. Barney kneels beside Frank. The old man lies sprawled by the sink, with his eyes closed. He's still breathing.

"You're just in time to make it a real party, Leaky-leaky." Darnell doesn't look too steady. I know what a guy looks like when he's flying, and Darnell's nearing the clouds. He also holds a gun. "Now I'll find out if she really is your girl. Whose brains do I blow out first, yours or hers?"

Blood drips on the floor around my feet. Barney leaves Frank and starts for me.

"I didn't say you could move," Darnell snarls.

"He's bleeding." She points at the stain on my sleeve.

"He'll do a lot more than that soon. Now, get back."

She leaves me and backs up to the stove. Why didn't she get closer to the back wall where her purse hangs on a hook? Did she ever get the pepper spray she once talked about? Maybe I could get across the room, open the gallon bag purse. Fish inside through all the girl-stuff until I find the canister, whip it out and use it on these guys before I get hit, knifed, or shot. *Excuse me guys, would you step aside and let me get to the girl's purse so I can paw inside, pull out the weapon, be a hero, and save the day?* Yeah, that'll happen. Maybe Frank is just faking and will jump to his feet and use a little army Kung Fu on them. Maybe someone will step in my blood and fall and help even the odds. Maybe my phone drop-dialed 911 by itself when it fell.

No, maybe's about it. Barney, Frank, and I are all in deep shit.

Barney stares at me. I cannot, will not, let anything happen to her.

I turn to Lamont. "You have to know this isn't worth it."

"This whole plan was stupid." Lamont sounds anxious and looks confused, like none of this was his idea and he wants out. Guess he still doesn't realize he has no real power, not with someone like Darnell, ready to snatch anything. Including his life.

"You don't matter, you and your big ideas." Darnell waves the gun in the air. "I'm in charge, you little prick. From now on, I do what the hell I please. I'll be the one bringing the Enforcers back to the top. No smart-aleck boy is bossing me around anymore."

The other guys talk smack, apparently not caring which one is their boss. Barney looks at me. When our eyes meet, she shifts her head slightly. I follow her gaze to the nearby coffee machine. She glances back at me.

I nod. We'll only have one chance.

"This is stupid," Lamont says. He walks toward Darnell. "Give me the gun."

Darnell fires. Lamont throws himself to the ground.

Life-In-The-Hood lesson: when you see a chance, go for it.

I lunge at Darnell and get in that all-important first blow. The gun goes off again, a bullet whistles past my head. I collide with him and my momentum carries us both across the room. The sound of a splash, breaking glass, and screams come from behind me. I drive Darnell's head against the wall. Darnell's fist hits my injured shoulder, an arm grown tough from hundreds of Granddad's blows. The new pain means nothing. His other hand goes for my throat. No gun, a part of me realizes. The rest of me keeps fighting. My fist connects with his mouth. His groan joins the sounds coming from behind me. I grab his arms and twist them behind him.

The gun goes off again.

There's a clang as bullet hits metal, followed by a pot falling from a shelf.

I keep hold of Darnell and turn to look behind me. Three Enforcers lie on the ground, two of them covering their faces and writhing in pain on a floor wet with hot coffee. Frank stands over one. Barney has her fist cocked, about to drive it into another's face. Lamont stands at the door, holding the smoking gun.

"Shoot this sucker, then lets get out of here," Darnell tells Lamont.

"If I shoot anyone, it will be you," Lamont says. He turns to me. "I guess I'm as dumb as you thought I was."

*

When the police arrive, Lamont drops the gun and lets them handcuff him without protest. Darnell and the others growl and bluster as they, too, are cuffed and taken away.

I sit on a hospital bed in a small cubicle surrounded by machines and separated from the rest of the emergency room by a green vinyl curtain. I would be embarrassed by the faded hospital gown they put me in after the paramedics undressed me, but Barney's checking out my legs, so I don't mind.

"You like my bod that much?" I ask, ignoring the nurse working on my shoulder. Six stitches; not the worst I've ever had.

"You've been stabbed again; how can you laugh?"

"Everyone knows I'm too bad to be hurt."

Barney crosses her arms over her chest. "I suppose you'll want me to keep this a secret, too?"

I think about the cops, the paramedics, and Frank. I shake my head. There's no chance this will remain a secret. "No, tell the world. I can't wait for David to hear." I wonder if saving his sister will count as an amends to him? The dude will flip out when he realizes how much he owes me. Not the most worthy thought, but hey, I shed blood.

"David keeps blowing up my phone with texts warning me to keep away from you. I love him, but he makes me so mad when he tries to boss me around."

"What about me? What do I make you?"

"I'm still figuring that out." She scrunches her nose as she speaks. "Being around you used to make me so furious I wanted to scream, until I realized I was really mad at myself for letting a hot guy become more important than anything else."

Hot guy? "How hot?"

"Don't make me tell you the real truth." She tries to sound tough, but her grin makes my stomach tighten.

"Then I'll tell you, you sizzle. Do I have any chance at all?"

"To be my boyfriend? I already told you that can't happen." She sighs and turns away, her head bent. "I really wanted to hate you."

"Oh. I got that."

"But I can't." She turns back and her face is all smiles. She holds out a hand. "You and I can move forward, too. As friends."

"Friends." I take her hand and we shake. Her skin is warm and soft. Friendship. Not exactly what I'm looking for. But it's a start.

One day at a time, right?

*

I had to go through a school assembly, with Henderson choking as he called me a hero. I don't know which of us hated that the most. But the most important part was sitting next to my dad and hearing him say, "I'm proud of you, Son."

Now I stand in the hall of a church, watching as Zach and his friends troop inside to the AA meeting room. Dad has a meeting at the other end of the hall. Al-Anon. He's going to cut his own God-complex down to size and learn to live with someone like me in his life.

I stuff my copy of the *Big Book of Alcoholics Anonymous* under my arm and step through the door to join Zach and the group.

RESOURCES

There is help if you or a loved one have problems related to alcohol, drugs or mood disorders. You don't have to suffer alone.

AA (Alcoholics Anonymous) - http://www.aa.org

ACOA (Adult Children Of Alcoholics) - http://www.adultchildren.org/

Families Anonymous, for friends and family members struggling with loved ones who have problems of addiction or mental illness - http://familiesanonymous.org/

Alanon (for adults) and Alateen for families dealing with an alcoholic member - http://al-anon.alateen.org/home

NA (Narcotics Anonymous) - http://www.na.org

Depression and Bipolar support alliance - http://www.dbsalliance.org

ACKNOWLEDGEMENTS

Big thanks to the members of Illinois Society of Children's Book Writers and Illustrators for their continued encouragement; and to the members of both the Chicago North and Wisconsin chapters of Romance Writers of America for critiques and encouragement, and the examples their members provided.

To Mary Jo Lepo, who continues to have faith in me and gives me a push when I need one. And to Jim Elgas, who invited me to submit to *The Arlington Almanac* and published my very first short story.

SNEAK PEEK

Neill Mallory has a good life with his older bother. He has a bright future as a doctor. He has friends. But there's a new teacher giving him grief and showing too much interest in him. Neill thought being gay was his biggest problem, until the teacher turns up dead and his brother is the number one suspect.

Worst still, Neill discovers that he is considered the motive for his brother's act. He has to team up with the teacher's daughter to find the real killer if he's going to save his family.

Minority of One

ISBN 978-0-9881821-2-7
Coming in 2013 from B. A. Binns and

AllTheColorsOfLove.

Like AllTheColorsOfLove on Facebook

MINORITY OF ONE

I was six the first time Mom called me a contrarian, and couldn't even pronounce the word. Now I'm proud of that title. It explains why I have French fourth period instead of the Spanish class that most of the students at Farrington sign up for.

Spanish is practically this neighborhood's second language. An easy ace for guys needing a GPA boost, a relaxation period for those who don't. The school is thirty-five percent Hispanic. We've got Mexican, Puerto Rican, even a little Cuban, and don't you dare mix up which is which. I didn't learn Spanish at home, but I picked up my share on the playground from guys who did. I swear as fluently in Spanish as I do in English. Better. Mom never punished me for the Spanish swears she didn't understand, so I learned to say *chinga* or *culero*.

French opened up a whole new world. I've added *câlisse* and *trou du cul* to my vocabulary.

As I approach maze they call the language section, I see the new girl standing in the hall. She's a new addition to our school's white population, with skin so pale I bet she's never had a tan. She could be a ninja in the black sweater, black pants, and blonde hair pulled back in an old-lady bun. The girl has to be making some kind of statement.

Blondie stands like a rock in the middle of a river, forcing the little fish to swirl around her. As I watch, one dude stops to say something to her. Whatever it is makes her head snap up and earns him a back-the-hell-off glare.

"You really want to be castrated?" she says. "Or are you just testing?"

"Bitch," echoes through the hall as he hitches his pants and walks away from her toward me. "You and butch belong together," he mutters as he comes close. Not too close, he's careful not to intrude into the no-touch zone most male students draw around me.

Generally I like girls. They're practically the only friends I have. But even though it's her first day, I've already seen Blondie in action. She walked into my first period class and turned up her nose at Wendy a.k.a. boyfriend thief. I could have called this girl my sister from another mother after the way she cut Wendy down. Only that was just the start. She was mean to everyone, including poor Mrs. Petit who really wants to believe in that you-can-do-anything-if-you-try and we-should-all-be-friends mishmash my parents used to try to make me accept.

I'm okay with this girl keeping her nose in the air and pretending I don't exist. The designated gay guy already has enough problems with life.

Her head swings to me and for a second our eyes meet. She doesn't look triumphant. Just alone. Thanks to her killer image, no one is even looking at her now. Her shoulders lift briefly before she goes back to studying the paper in her hands.

I walk closer and see she's holding a map of the school. The one they hand out to freshmen and transfers. One of the most useless things ever invented. Whoever put this building together never talked to the man who drew the map. You get lost far quicker with that excuse for a guide than with a blindfold.

I almost keep going. But *câlisse*, she looks really lost. And if there's any class I can afford to be late to, it's French. The Principal has been promising us a new teacher since Mr. Faber suddenly retired. There aren't a lot of spare French teachers available in the middle of a semester. Fewer still with so little seniority the teacher's union will force them to transfer down to our end of the city at a moment's notice. We've had to deal with a string of useless subs.

"Can I help you find something?" I ask as I stop by her side.

Her green eyes widen, almost like she's seeing a ghost or some other beastie that doesn't belong in the real world. "I can't believe there's really a gentleman in this place."

"If you shook off the chip you might find a lot of us."

That makes her jaw tighten. A moment later she amazes me by nodding. "Sorry. I guess if I knew what I was doing in this world, I probably wouldn't be such a bitch."

That's probably closer to an apology than she's given in a long time. "What world are you from?"

"You don't want to know."

She could be right. "What are you looking for?"

"The language classrooms. I found room one seventeen, but that's the language lab."

"You went the right way then. The map's just tricky. Come on, I'm going there myself. I'll show you where they hide the classes." As she follows me down the hall, I explain. "You have to go through the lab and past the teacher's offices. There should be a letter next to your room. What's it say?"

"One seventeen D."

Her head is bent as she stuffs the folded map into her pocket, so she doesn't see me stop. She's several steps past me before she notices I'm not with her and turns.

"I thought you were a freshman," I said. That's how Mrs. Petit introduced her. I don't even remember her name, just how surprised I felt to have a new student, and a freshman, enter our physics class in the middle of February.

"Yes, I guess I am," she says.

"In third year French?"

Another head bob.

"That's my class."

She shrugs like it's no big deal. I suppose she's right. Coincidences do happen. Besides, we're here.

A woman stands by the instructor's desk. Tall, blond, pale-skinned, slim in a well-cut, and very expensive, gray pantsuit. Her blond hair is badly cut, almost hacked. Except for her eyes being a smoky gray instead of green, she looks enough like Blondie to be her sister.

Or her mother.

Something tells me this isn't just another substitute.

"*Bonjour.*" The woman in the totally out-of-place dark velvet suit smiles at us and points to two empty chairs in the front row. "*S'il vous plaisez.*"

Blondie sucks in a deep breath. She looks like she'd disappear if she could. Since she can't, she drops into one of the chairs and stares straight ahead. As I take the seat beside her she mutters, "Welcome to my world."

ABOUT THE AUTHOR

 B. A. Binns, winner of the 2010 National Readers Choice award in the Young Adult category, and finalist in the Romance Writers of America Golden Heart ®, is an adoptive parent and cancer survivor. She has degrees from both Roosevelt University and DePaul University. She writes stories told from a teen boy's point of view to show "real boys growing into real men...and the people who love them."

She is a member of Romance Writers of America, Society of Children's Book Writers and Illustrators, the American Library Association, ALAN (Assembly on Literature for Adolescents of NCTE), and YALSA (the Young Adult Library Services Association). Her short stories are frequently published in the Arlington Almanac. She gives presentations at schools, libraries and writer's conferences. Visit her website to see short stories and excerpts from future books coming from AllTheColorsOfLove press.

Connect with the author on
Goodreads: http://www.goodreads.com/BABinns
Twitter: http://twitter.com/barbarabinns
Facebook: http://facebook.com/allthecolorsoflove
Blog: http://barbarabinns.com
Email: binns@babinns.com

CPSIA information can be obtained at www.ICGtesting.com
Printed in the USA
LVOW11s1906181016

509270LV00003B/506/P